"WE'VE GOT TO DEAL
between us," Rick said, reaching to cover one
of her hands with his to keep her from moving away.

"What do you suggest?" Bryn asked in a whisper. With a deliciously slow sweep of her sable
lashes, she cautiously looked up at his mouth, then
met his gaze.

Running the backs of his fingers under her
chin, he lifted it as he lowered his head. From
the corner of his eye he could see her curl her
fingers into the key lime pie, then lift a gob from
the plate. Shifting his weight, he leaned closer and
suggested the wrong thing. "You wouldn't."

As her hand arced through the air, he caught
her wrist and sent a splatter onto the sleeve of his
jacket. Ignoring the mess, he brought her hand
to his mouth and began licking her fingers. After
trying to pull her hand away once, she gave up,
her gaze riveted on his lips and tongue.

Letting go of her, he stepped back and stripped
off his jacket. "I think it'd be better if I showed
you," he said, his hands going to the back of her
neck and his fingers slipping into her hair. "Open
your mouth. It'll be easier that way."

"I don't know—"

"I do."

"But—"

"Captain's orders."

Her lips parted at his whispered command. . . .

WHAT ARE *LOVESWEPT* ROMANCES?

They are stories of true romance and touching emotion. We believe those two very important ingredients are constants in our highly sensual and very believable stories in the LOVESWEPT line. Our goal is to give you, the reader, stories of consistently high quality that may sometimes make you laugh, sometimes make you cry, but are always fresh and creative and contain many delightful surprises within their pages.

Most romance fans read an enormous number of books. Those they truly love, they keep. Others may be traded with friends and soon forgotten. We hope that each LOVESWEPT romance will be a treasure—a "keeper." We will always try to publish

LOVE STORIES YOU'LL NEVER FORGET
BY AUTHORS YOU'LL ALWAYS REMEMBER

The Editors

CAPTAIN'S ORDERS

SUSAN CONNELL

BANTAM BOOKS

NEW YORK · TORONTO · LONDON · SYDNEY · AUCKLAND

CAPTAIN'S ORDERS

A Bantam Book / July 1994

ISBN 0-553-44439-5

Published simultaneously in the United States and Canada

Bantam Books are published by Bantam Books, a division of Bantam Dou-
bleday Dell Publishing Group, Inc. Its trademark, consisting of the words
"Bantam Books" and the portrayal of a rooster, is Registered in U.S. Patent
and Trademark Office and in other countries. Marca Registrada. Bantam
Books, 1540 Broadway, New York, New York 10036.

PRINTED IN THE UNITED STATES OF AMERICA

OPM   0 9 8 7 6 5 4 3 2 1

To Captain Jim Connell—thanks for all those gaudy-awful sunsets.

And special thanks to the Hash House Harriers of Abidjan for inviting me to my first semiformal ball.
I still have my T-shirt!

PROLOGUE

"*Rrrrawk!* Repent, you sinner. Repent. Repent!"

Rick Parrish wanted more time to take in the sights and sounds of Pappy's Crab Shack, to imprint them indelibly in his memory so that he could recall them at will during the next two weeks. Now that Miss Scarlett had squawked his arrival into the second-story open-air bar, his private moment of fortification had ended. The regulars sent him a barrage of wolf whistles and catcalls, letting him know they'd seen him. And his suit. Reaching past the Flesh-Eating Killer Bird sign, Rick adjusted the parrot's red-ribboned boater.

"What'll it be, Captain Parrish?" Pappy Madison asked from inside the wraparound bar.

More heads turned in Rick's direction as he pretended serious consideration of the question. Pappy's query was the same every evening, and so was Rick's response. Half the patrons in the Florida Keys bar chorused the answer along with him.

"Cold beer, conch fritters, and a gaudy-awful sunset, Pappy!"

"Can do," Pappy said, pulling a frosted mug from the cooler.

Weaving his way through the crowded establishment, Rick exchanged several irreverent greetings as he headed toward his usual place by the west rail. He spotted one of his marina employees with his arms resting on the tanned shoulders of two attentive blondes. Jiggy Latham winked, flashing two victory signs before lowering his head to receive a kiss from one of the girls. Rick walked on by, trying for a fleeting moment to remember what it was like to be so young. When he reminded himself that he was barely thirty-four, he hid a halfhearted chuckle in a hasty look around the room.

A few tourists were trying hard to blend in with the locals. If their unfamiliar faces hadn't given them away, the scent of their suntan lotions, the sight of their sunburns, and the fruity daiquiris they ordered certainly would have. He glanced at his watch, then folded his suit jacket and laid it over a chair. With his luggage stowed in the back of his Jeep, a plane ticket in his suit pocket, and the almost desperate desire to drink in the bar's atmosphere, he felt like a tourist himself.

He looked at his watch again. He had fifteen minutes to immerse himself in the convivial din before he headed for the airport. Fifteen minutes in an open-air bar that had become more welcoming to him than his own living room. And if all that weren't enough to draw him here, this place didn't have ghosts. But he didn't want to think about that right now. One of the waitresses was pulling the plug on the jukebox, cutting off a Motown classic. Before the protests could reach a rioting level, Pappy banged his hand on the bar.

"Behave yourselves," Pappy warned. "The show's about to begin."

The show, Rick noted with pleasure, had begun in the late afternoon when the sun, ballooning with color, began drifting down to the water. Pappy's patrons assembled for the last act. The grand finale. Chairs scraped the rough plank floor as they were turned toward the west rail. And then, as always, there was a moment of silence when everyone seemed to hold a collective breath. Rick never tired of the dazzling spectacle, a mixture of gaudy melodrama and ancient dignity.

As the show continued, good-natured laughter and the clink of glasses filled the balmy air. Over in another corner Tweed MacNeil lifted his guitar, perched himself on a stool, and teased the audience with a few familiar notes.

"Do it to me, Tweed," a thirtyish woman begged, and "Margaritaville" rolled out rich and mellow under the thatched roof.

Miss Scarlett joined in, exclaiming in a gravelly voice, "Make a joyful noise!"

After a while Pappy showed up at Rick's elbow and slipped a basket of conch fritters in front of him. He followed the neat presentation by thunking down two full mugs of beer, their foamy heads sloshing over the tops and onto the table. "Think I'll join you."

"I'm going to miss this, Pappy," Rick said, palming the foam away from the table edge then flicking it over the rail.

"That's right," Pappy said, wiping his hands on his shorts before taking the chair next to Rick. "You're flying up to Philadelphia tonight to see Angie's folks. No wonder you're dressed like . . . you're dressed." He strained for a look at Rick's lap. "Didn't get any on you, did I?"

Rick gave the old man an easy laugh. "No. I've been coming to this place long enough to know when to move out of the way."

As Pappy's eyes met his, the old man's voice lost its bantering tone. "How long has it been since Angie died?"

"Five years," he said quickly, reaching for the beer and taking a sip. Five years since he'd been coming to Pappy's alone. Keeping his eyes straight ahead, he cleared his throat when he sensed Pappy was about to ask another question. Too soon he'd be bombarded by memories of Angie, and right now all he wanted was to enjoy his beer, Pappy's atmosphere, and one more gaudy-awful sunset. He eased back in his chair and looked around him.

Several tourists had set up cameras on the rail and were snapping their shutter buttons in a manic move to capture the moment. Rick watched, keenly aware of their need to have a piece of the place to take away with them. He blew softly through pursed lips, hoping to ease the strange sensations in his chest. This wasn't *his* only sunset at Pappy's. Still, in the pinkish-gold tint bathing Coconut Key, he was never more aware of the earth rolling closer to twilight. Rick shifted in his chair, releasing his stranglehold on the worn wooden armrests. What the hell was he so uptight about? Unless there was a major hurricane about to hit the Keys, Pappy's Crab Shack would be here when he got back.

"My granddaughter's coming for a visit."

"I think you mentioned she was," Rick said, turning to his friend with a grateful smile. He was relieved to talk about something else. "Don't think I've met her. Have I?"

"Bryn? You'd remember Bryn if you met her. Come to think of it, she always comes down here when you're up in Philadelphia." With a proud shake of his head, Pappy concluded, "She's a pistol."

"A pistol, huh?" Crossing his arms, he leaned them on the damp table. "Too bad I'll miss her."

Pappy lifted the front of his fisherman's cap and scratched his head. "Another time," he said, as the sun, accompanied by a trilling flourish from Tweed MacNeil's guitar, disappeared below the horizon.

"Another time," Rick said, reaching for his wallet.

Pappy waved off Rick's motion. "Put your money away. It's on the house tonight."

"Take care, then," Rick said, knowing his grin was all the thank-you Pappy would accept.

A few minutes later he was headed north on U.S. Highway 1, fiddling with the radio and already counting the days until he could return.

ONE

Rick Parrish was going home.

Tugging at the knot in his tie, he loosened it a few more inches, then unbuttoned another button on his shirt. He couldn't wait until he stored these clothes, pulled on his jeans, and started the yearly process of putting his memories of Angie a little further back in his heart. The annual visit with her parents never got easier, but this year's visit was finally over.

He strained for his first glimpse of the Keys' mile marker, and stepped down on the accelerator the moment he saw it. Like a white bullet, his Jeep sped onto the last bridge before home. Two weeks away from Coconut Key was two weeks too long. *And he was so close now, he could smell it.*

The first thing he was going to do was have a frosty mug of beer at Pappy's Crab Shack. After that, he'd check on his marina. Life was beginning to feel right again. Tapping out the rhythm of "Margaritaville" on his steering wheel, he drove off the bridge and onto the highway. That "almost home" feeling settled over him, as familiar and welcoming as his chair at Pappy's. He turned up the volume on his tape, and the smile that had been threatening to surface for the last two hours eased across his face.

Turning onto Marina Road, he hit his horn twice, announcing his return to the group he knew was gathered at Pappy's. A roiling cloud of dust followed him into Pappy's empty parking lot.

Rick's smile left his face before he had a chance to jam his foot on the brake. Yanking off his sunglasses, he waved away the dust billowing over him and stared slack-jawed through the windshield.

He was hallucinating.

He had to be, because Pappy's Crab Shack had been here two weeks ago and now it was gone. Or at least the peeling paint was gone, and being replaced with a second coat of banana yellow. He recognized the painter. Tweed should have been inside along with the two men who were hanging a new sign.

CHEZ MADISON
DISTINCTIVE CUISINE IN THE HEART OF THE KEYS
OPENING SOON

"Tweed!" Rick shouted, switching off the ignition. "What the hell's going on?"

Gesturing with his paintbrush, the man on the ladder said, "Plenty. And you're not going to like any of it." Tweed winked. "Well, maybe a bit of it. But you go inside and find out for yourself."

Rick vaulted out of the Jeep. His momentary shock was turning into an uncomfortable tingle across his shoulders. What was Pappy Madison up to? Striding across the parking lot and onto a newly laid, petunia-lined brick walkway, he felt a growing sense of apprehension.

When his foot landed on the first step, he hesitated, then slowly tested the next step. The creak was gone. A disgusted snort left his nostrils. The entire set of steps had been replaced. So had the shaky handrail. Taking the steps two at a time, he crested the top one, stepped inside the bar, and choked back a groan.

It was worse than he could have imagined. The beer-stained floors had been sanded clean, the rickety tables removed, and the naked mermaid mural blotted out with more of that banana-yellow paint.

What horror was next? he wondered, scanning the room.

The ultimate insult struck him like a boom in the chest. The dark pine captain's chair, which everyone on Coconut Key knew to be his, his poker chair, the chair that held him while he bragged about his fishing, the chair he'd passed out in a few too many times, was splattered with paint and shoved in a corner like a piece of discarded history. His heart sank, then rebounded to its rightful place, bringing with it a need for an explanation . . . and a burning desire for retribution against the perpetrator of the blasphemous act.

"Pappy, get your sorry ass out here before I—" Rick's words blended with those of a willowy redhead who was backing through the kitchen door with an armload of cloth napkins.

"All deliveries through the back entrance, please," she was saying. "And could you—oh!"

He'd startled her, but no more than she'd startled him. In that swelling moment of silence Rick took her in, front and back, with the aid of a new wall mirror. She was sleek yet curvy, with an aura of sophistication he sensed instantly. Hell, her trendy hairstyle alone could have told him that. The feathery fullness of it appeared to defy gravity, framing her shocked expression with what looked like auburn sunbursts. He wasn't surprised when she blinked first. Under the weight of her thick, curly lashes, it was a wonder her eyes hadn't closed before he took note of their clear amber color.

"Pappy's not here," she said regarding his empty hands with cautious interest. When she let go of the napkins, most of them fell into a basket at her feet. "I'm his granddaughter, Bryn Madison."

His gaze followed her ladylike yet provocative stoop near his feet. As she gathered up the napkins from the floor, he watched her cropped top move up and down her back. He'd seen hundreds, maybe thousands of women in skimpy bathing suits, but this peekaboo view of her flesh was different. Every movement was an invitation to touch her right *there* at the base of her spine. Each time she reached, he dug his nails into his palms and hoped it was the last time. He gave himself permission to breathe after she tossed the last napkin into the basket she had perched on her hip. Rising, she smiled and extended her hand as if nothing had happened.

And nothing had. Yet.

Rick had seen her type at his marina. Just brimming with gracious enthusiasm until the first fishhook had to be baited or the first stiff breeze destroyed the hairdo. Take-your-breath-away beauty or not, he told himself to expect much of the same from this one. He was never wrong about these things.

Then she touched him.

Her perfectly manicured hand slipped into his, her fingertips wrapping around the side, before gripping him in a capable hold. She gave one solid shake that told him his theory didn't apply to her. No dead fish here. This was a live one. With each passing second her touch sent him more disconcerting messages. Confident. Competent. Assertive. Challenging.

Threatening. Threatening? Where had that idea come from? Where had any of those ideas come from? He knew nothing about her except that Bryn rhymed with win, and that she smelled like cool cream and cinnamon. "I'm Rick Parrish," he said, in a raspy voice he didn't recognize as his own. He cleared his throat.

"Is there something I can help you with, Rick?"

He was sure there was something, but he couldn't remember what that something was. He was far too busy trying to figure out why her spirited handshake and blended scent were still knocking him off his center. That dead-calm center he guarded with his life. The reason had to be more than Bryn Madison's confident smile and the self-assured way she jutted her hip to brace the basket. His gaze strayed to the mirror behind her, giving him a periscopic view of the way her short skirt curved so lovingly around her hips. Round, firm hips that made his palms itch. She reminded him of Pappy's mermaid mural. In fact, she could have been the model for the mural.

Rick fought the temptation to totally immerse himself in the mirror's stolen view of her backside. Of course, he wasn't breaking any law by looking. Even so, he knew he was asking for trouble if he didn't quit it—right after he compared Bryn's backside to the mermaid's. Turning toward the wall, he bit down and exhaled sharply. He'd been staring at Bryn's body for so long, he'd forgotten that the mermaid mural no longer existed.

With that thought burning in his brain, he looked back at her. *She* was the cause of this. And the reason adrenaline was roaring through his body. He watched her as she riffled through the whites and pastels in the basket, and followed her to the bar.

"If you're looking for a job bartending or as a cook, I'm afraid we're not—"

"I'm not looking for work. I want to know what's going on. And where's Pappy?" he asked, losing the battle to keep his voice all business.

She stopped her riffling and looked up at him. Her lips lifted at the corners into a proud grin that made his stomach flip-flop. Damn it to hell. If he wasn't going to fixate on her perfectly curved behind, neither was he going to get hung up on her mouth. Her lush, red mouth smiling in a way that was adding confusion to his growing list of complaints.

"What's going on here is a much-needed remodeling. And none too soon," she said, with a don't-you-agree tilt of her head. "Pappy's still in the hospital, so we won't be able to reopen until—"

"Hold on right there," he said, turning an ear in her direction. That cold and queasy feeling started in his gut when he heard the word *hospital*. "Run that one by me again. What's Pappy doing in the hospital?"

"He broke his leg when his foot went through a rotted step. Of course, I immediately rebuilt both staircases. Then I started right in on the rest of the place."

A sharp, sibilant curse left Rick's lips, causing her eyebrows to lift and hold. He shook his head in a halfhearted apology, but more to clear it of those images of Angie. Those images that he'd fooled himself into thinking were gone for another year. "Is she . . . ?" He closed his eyes to make the moment disappear, but he knew in the same instant that certain things never would. "I mean, is he going to be okay?"

"The orthopedic surgeon's assured me Grandfather will be fine, but he'll have to stay in the hospital over on Marathon for a few more weeks. Are you a regular customer of his?"

"I'm his friend. I own Parrish's Marina. I do fishing-boat charters." Lifting his chin in the direction of the north rail and its view of the marina, he waited until she had a look. "I've been away," he said.

"Rick Parrish. Of course. I've been preparing the box lunches for your charters since Grandfather's accident. I'd love to take a boat ride one of these days when I'm not so busy. Maybe—"

"What happened to Linda and Susan? Why aren't they doing the lunches?"

"The waitresses? I'm afraid I had to let them go. They've gotten work at a resort over on Islamorada. I think it's called Conch Castle. If they're still interested, I'll consider rehiring them when we reopen. In the meantime," she said, "life must go on."

"So I've been told," he murmured, looking around the room again, then throwing up his hands. "This is unbelievable."

"I know. I hadn't taken a good look at the place in quite a while, so when I walked in this time, I couldn't believe how things had deteriorated," she said with a disapproving roll of her eyes. Placing the basket on the bar, she pulled out a white napkin, picked off its price sticker, and began folding it.

She wasn't getting it. But she would. He shifted his weight from one leg to the other and considered her blissful ignorance. He could be patient. As soon as she stopped fooling around with that napkin and started paying attention to him, he would tell her how things worked around here. By the way she was concentrating on the napkin, it wouldn't be any time soon. He could be very patient.

He watched the precise way she was rolling, folding and tucking the cloth until, turning it over, she smoothed it for what he hoped was the last time. Her nails made a line of cherry red ovals when she pressed her slender fingers against the white cloth. His thoughts strayed to the kind of attention she could pay to him with those fingers. Those exquisitely feminine, deftly moving fingers that were turning a plain piece of material into a three-dimensional work of art. Concentrating on her hands, he indulged himself in a few seconds of erotic fantasies. The provocative ideas stirred his blood with shocking speed.

"See what a little inspiration and perspiration can do?" she asked, holding up the napkin she had folded to resemble a bird. She jiggled it, making its wings flap. "A miracle."

"Yes, but can it clean up after itself?" he asked, hoping she'd pick up on the tinge of sarcasm in his voice. She didn't. Her soft laughter volleyed his sentiment back to him, making him feel contrite. Or more to the point, plain nasty for trying to bring her down when all she wanted was to share a lighthearted moment with him. He'd turned away too many opportunities for lighthearted moments, but this one felt different.

"While we're on the subject of birds, where's Miss Scarlett?"

"A Mr. Latham volunteered to take her until things are a bit more settled here. And that won't be too much longer once I pitch the rest of that stuff and the new furniture is delivered," she said, pointing to the battered furniture and dusty beer signs piled in the corner. Leaning her elbows on the edge of the bar, she dropped her chin on her laced fingers and turned her face to his. "Amazing what a bit of elbow grease and determination can accomplish in so little time, isn't it?"

"Amazing?" He tested the sandpapery texture of his chin, running the back of his hand across it, then down over his Adam's apple. "You could put it that way," he said, his gaze straying over her. He told himself he wasn't interested in the way her hair moved when she looked into the basket, or the way her eyes got all dreamy when she was talking about the place. Or even the way the toe of her one shoe balanced behind the other. And he was especially not interested in the way she was again rolling another napkin beneath her flattened fingers, then manipulating the ridged hem to produce some desired effect that was making her smile again. He was mad. And more than slightly aroused, which made him madder still.

Straightening up, she reached into the basket and exchanged her half-folded white napkin for an apricot one. Looking pleased with her selection, she flicked the folds from the napkin, spread it out on the bar, and began again.

"Color is so important in setting the right mood, don't you agree?" Her cautious look returned when he didn't speak. "Well, you do agree that Pappy's Crab Shack needed a face-lift, don't you?"

"What you've got going here is much more than a face-lift," Rick said, unable to keep the emotion out of his voice. "Pappy's going to have a fit when he sees the place."

Her laughter rippled through him like an unexpected shiver.

"Pappy is not going to have a fit, Rick. He's given me carte blanche to do over the Crab Shack." Pushing away from the bar, she motioned with her hands. "My speciality is hotel restaurant design. I usually have to work within established parameters on those jobs. Now, I'm not saying I don't appreciate the discipline, but no one is telling me what to do this time."

She stopped to look at him, giving him an exuberant smile. He fought the urge to smile back. She didn't appear to notice his tight-lipped expression as she continued telling him about her plans to ruin Pappy's.

"It's going to be stunning. Light and airy. Lots of twisted lace valances above the window openings. A wedding-cake trim on top of these luscious walls." She wrinkled her nose in dismay. "That is, when I can find someone to do a drop ceiling. I'm willing to keep it a tad tropical, but I'm aiming for mostly French country. Oh, and there will definitely be a wine bar to replace that mess," she said, waving off the area where rows of rum, gin, and assorted liquors used to be.

Rick watched her move around the room, pointing out more changes to come. Once she got on a roll, her energy was astonishing. With each new idea, he felt his world rushing toward extinction.

"I'll limit the menu at first. No more than four entrées. And no peanut shells anywhere. I found peanut shells in the rest rooms. Can you imagine?" Clapping her hands together, she brought them under her chin, then turned back toward him. Suddenly she looked as if she'd tripped on something. "Why are you looking at me like that?"

He slipped his sunglasses on the moment she began stroking that place below her breasts. It should have been easy enough to look at something else, anything else, but he couldn't stop watching her touching herself that way. One moment she was posturing and talking like a madame president, and the next she reminded him of an excited kid at summer camp. The first image was as intriguing as the second was poignant. He adjusted his sunglasses, thankful that they prevented her from knowing that he continued to stare at that place between her breasts, wishing he could stroke it too.

"Did you say that Pappy hit his head?" he asked, taking off his suit jacket and tossing it on the bar.

"No." Lowering her hand to her hip, she gave him a quick and suspicious once-over. Her wistful moment dissolved, replaced with that instructive tone he was already beginning to hate. "I told you, his foot went through a rotted step."

"I think he hit his head," Rick said, nodding as if he had just been convinced of it. "Yes, ma'am," he continued, walking over to where his old chair was and dragging it out into the center of the room. Sitting down, he lifted his feet to rest them on the sawhorse, then folded his arms. "As a matter of fact, I think Pappy must have whacked it good and hard to let you do this to his place. Bryn, take my word for it. This distinctive, lace-valance cuisine idea isn't going to work."

Bryn Madison stared hard at the broad-shouldered man relaxing in the battered captain's chair. She pressed her lips together, fighting back the urge to pull in a sharp breath. Rick Parrish was arrogant, opinionated, and not a little antagonistic. Those things alone should have been reason enough to dismiss him, but there was something else about the man that stopped her from telling him to get out. Forget that he possessed the most effective packaging for testosterone she'd even seen. Forget that his permanent tan, his sun-streaked hair, and his handsome face, made all the more handsome with its weathered touches, had been inviting her stares since the moment she'd seen him. And forget that his own blue-eyed gaze had her warm and tingly and strangely alert. All of it, she told herself, was nothing but an overblown reaction to the man's overpowering presence. The most fascinating thing about Rick Parrish was his passion and the way he was trying to hide it. And the fact that he couldn't.

She watched as he stripped off his tie and began rolling it into a neat bundle. When he stuffed it into one of his trouser pockets, he strained the open V of his shirt, giving her a peek at his curly chest hair. Without warning, she found herself picturing him unbuttoning his shirt and tugging it off to reveal a light and springy mat of hair covering a supremely masculine chest. A chest to stroke. Tickle. Kiss. And when he opened his arms and whispered her name, a warm and waiting chest for her to press her face against. The mesmerizing images continued until she pressed her fingers to her forehead and willed them to stop.

"Bryn, honey," he said, flicking an imaginary piece of lint from his knee, "I know what I'm talking about. You're wasting your time and Pappy's money. Open your eyes and stop this before we can't fix it. You're making a big mistake."

For one shattering moment all she could focus on was his casually delivered endearment. Honey. She hadn't heard that word since her last close relationship. Maybe it wasn't her fiancé's fault that the excitement he generated was usually one-sided. His side. But she hadn't had a problem tossing the ring in his face when he'd accused her of loving her career more than she loved him. That was three years ago, and although her biological clock wasn't clanging the alarm, she didn't like to be reminded of what she still lacked—a man to love and be loved by, a baby, and all those sweet endearments that came with the both of them. And now Rick Parrish, this man she hardly knew, tossed off "honey" in such a cavalier manner that it made her cheeks sting with angry heat. He was attempting to knock the wind out of her sails by telling her she couldn't handle a simple, albeit enjoyable, renovation for her grandfather. To top things off, he was also making it clear that her ideas were categorically wrong for Pappy's. She reached to smooth the buttons on her peplum jacket, but laced her trembling fingers together when she realized she'd removed it.

Rick Parrish wasn't going to get away with mocking her expertise. She'd kill him with kindness first!

"Well, Rick, honey, I disagree," she said, infusing her words with as much politeness as she could manage. "I think Coconut Key needs an upscale restaurant. Someplace special—"

"People can go to Key West if they want special," he said, lowering his feet to the floor. As if her work weren't worth a full wave of his hand, he lifted only his fingers to indicate her changes to the restaurant's interior. "But they don't want this kind of special. They want Pappy's."

"And how do you know what people want?" she asked, monitoring her composure with each strained word.

"Because I've lived here most of my life, and I know. What they want is a place where they can go and put their feet up, throw their peanut shells on the floor, and play the jukebox good and loud." Twisting around for a look at the back corner of the room, Rick did a double take, then came out of his chair, knocking it over in the awkward move. Pulling off his glasses, he dropped his voice to an unforgiving whisper. "What did you do with the jukebox?"

"I had it moved downstairs to the storage room. Someone's coming over from Grassy Key to look at it tonight." She leveled a look at him that was meant to tell him she wasn't backing down. "Does that meet with your approval?"

"You're selling Pappy's jukebox?" Before she could answer his question, he gestured toward the empty corner with his sunglasses. "That jukebox is not leaving Coconut Key," he said, his voice climbing again.

"Is that an order, Mr. Parrish, or an offer to buy it?" she asked. Picking up the basket of napkins, she walked calmly toward the kitchen door, her high heels making slow, soft tapping sounds. Once inside she waited for him, certain that he wasn't going to give up. Not like some men she'd had to stand up to in her career. Not with his fiery personality. Rick Parrish didn't disappoint her, and that made her feel all the more triumphant when she heard him approaching.

"It's the truth," he bellowed, slamming the door back against the kitchen wall.

Bryn set the basket on the butcher-block table, slid it back a few inches, and took a measured, calming breath before facing him again. She would have missed the tremor in his hand if she hadn't looked at the door first. He was holding his fingers flat against the wood panel, but lowered his arm when he stepped into the room. If this had been any other man, she would have been impressed with her ability to illicit such a show of emotion. But Rick Parrish had bypassed that kind of self-indulgent reaction and hit her where it mattered. In her reawakening libido. The burst of energy was invigorating. "You're walking around here like the man in charge, but you're not in charge. Not here anyway." She tapped the place between her breasts. "I am. And my eyes *are* open. This place was in desperate need of repair. The accident opened Grandfather's eyes too. He realizes it's time for a change. And I'm only too happy to be the instrument for that change."

"Change?" Shoving his sunglasses into his shirt pocket, he rested his hands on his hips and lifted his chin toward her. "Except for a few minor repairs, there wasn't a need for this much change. This is a local bar, for locals. Friends. Real people."

"I have no problem with that. They'll be more than welcome at Chez Madison," she said, folding her arms as she backed up and bumped into the butcher block. "As long as they dress appropriately."

"Look," he said, his voice searching for a reasoning tone. The muscles of his jaw twitched with effort. "I know these people and I know Pappy. I think you ought to stop all of this remodeling business and wait until Pappy sees how far overboard you've gone."

"Pappy knows what I have in mind. What I want to know is, what business is it of yours?"

"I'll tell you what business it is," he said, tapping his chest with his fingertips. "Anything that happens on Coconut Key is my business. I've seen too many of the Keys ruined by trendy resorts, seasonal spenders, and thoughtless entrepreneurs." Striding to the opposite side of the butcher block, he leaned over it toward her. "Lady, wake up. People here don't want or need your Chez Buffy fern grotto with its unpronounceable menu, expensive wine list, or," he said, taking a folded napkin from the basket, "these toy sailboats, for crissakes."

She tugged the napkin from his hand. "This one is not a sailboat."

"Well, pardon me. A bird."

"It's a party hat. But more importantly, it's made of cloth and has no dirty limericks printed on it." She made a face to lighten the tension, but he wasn't nibbling. Sighing audibly, she allowed a frown to replace her attempt at humor. "Can't you give Chez Madison a chance? I'm not closing the place, I'm simply giving it style."

"Pappy's Crab Shack had style," he said dryly.

"Well, now it will have a different style," she said as evenly as she could manage. "This key needs an upscale restaurant, and not only for the pleasure it will bring to the people living here. It's bound to attract tourists, seasonal residents, and perhaps locals from some of the other keys."

"More outsiders are not what we need around here."

"If it brings prosperity—"

"That remark just goes to show how little you know about this community. If people were interested in that kind of prosperity, they'd have sold their land to developers long before now."

"What is it specifically that bothers you about my changes?"

Rick shook his head. "Can't you see? You're setting up a situation here that Pappy won't be able to handle. He's an old man. He and his staff can boil crabs, tap a keg, and shoot the breeze. And that's about it, Bryn. Don't you care that you're going to set up this place, then leave him with more than he can handle?"

He'd sneered at her plans. He'd insulted her common sense. He'd even managed to steer her thoughts close to libidinous mutiny. But he wasn't going to get away with questioning her love for her grandfather.

"I would never do that to that dear man. I love him too much to ever allow such a catastrophe to happen."

"I'm not saying you don't love Pappy. You're simply not thinking this through from his angle." Pointing at her, he said, "And don't tell me you care about Coconut Key or its people, because you've already proved to me that you know nothing about them. There's a way of life here worth maintaining, Bryn. What you've got in mind will only disrupt it, and your venture will fail."

"Rick, we're only talking about a restaurant."

"No," he said, turning in frustration to slam his palm on the wall. "*You're* talking about a restaurant; *I'm* talking about a community institution. Pappy's Crab Shack is . . . is . . ." His words trailed off as he plowed his fingers through his hair, then reached for the edge of the block again.

He glared at her and failed to contain a low growl. And she glared back, certain that her eyelashes must be on fire. Rick Parrish was the most stubborn, most guarded, and most gorgeous man she'd ever met. And for any and all of those reasons, she wasn't giving in or giving up. Not now. Not later.

Tapping her nails on the wood surface, she slowly shook her head. "I still think there's something else you're not telling me. Besides your concern for Pappy and your devotion to the people of Coconut Key, what really bothers you about this?"

"What are you talking about?" he asked, eyeing her closely.

She started to circle him. As he turned his head to follow her with his eyes, Bryn watched his light brown hair play against his collar. When she was behind him, he gave up trying to look at her and took a deep breath instead. She was surprised that he held it so long. She sensed Rick Parrish wasn't the type to turn his back on many people. He most likely took things head on, yet she had managed to provoke him to a tense silence.

He continued holding his rigid posture, keeping the fabric of his shirt taut over his shoulder blades. The message he wanted to convey was lost in the truth she saw before her: Rick Parrish needed touching. The knowledge streaked through her like a tiny lightning bolt. But she wasn't going to touch him. She wasn't going to run her hands over the masculine delta of his back or trace the contours of his spine with her fingertips. Or her mouth. She felt for the back of her earring, pinching it hard enough to make an indentation on her thumb. Rubbing the mark, she silently applauded herself for removing the treacherous idea. She'd spent too many years building her professional reputation to commit such a rash act with a stranger. Walking around to the other side of him, she stayed close enough to see the muscles begin twitching in his jaw again.

"Rick, are there personal reasons—" She left off in midsentence when he jerked his head in her direction. Suddenly he was in charge of the moment, holding her in his dead-on gaze.

If he kept on staring like that, she would most definitely have to touch him to prevent herself from keeling against him. All five feet seven inches of her vibrating female form against his six-feet-plus wall of stubborn masculinity. And he would have to catch her in his arms, but he couldn't do that because he was folding them tightly across his chest.

Turning fully in her direction, he lowered his chin. Under other circumstances, he could have been lowering his head to kiss her, or inviting her to kiss him. From the intensity of his expression, she was certain kissing wasn't on his list of things to do to her. For one wild moment, she thought, *With lips like yours, it should be on your list of things to do to me*. The brazen idea had her cheeks scalding.

Rick considered pulling back from her, but he hadn't been near this much *life* in years. He closed his eyes long enough to remind himself about the important things in his world, and this woman was not one of them. "If you cared about Pappy, this place, and these people . . . but you don't."

She inched up closer to him. "But I *do*."

He lowered his face nearer hers. "The hell you do!"

"Will you please stop swearing?" she asked, scissoring her hands between them.

"Will you stop meddling?" he asked, countering her with his rising voice.

A third voice broke in, startling both of them to near-military attention.

"If you two cared any more about the people on this key, we'd all have to get earplugs."

Rick felt the breath rush from his lungs the second he realized who it was at the barroom door. Coconut Key's oldest cheerleader. "Hello, Liza. I didn't see you there."

"I'm not surprised," the gray-haired woman said before chuckling. "If you two can pull yourselves away from this engaging display of emotion and step out of the kitchen away from the knives, I'd like to talk with you."

He hadn't missed the not-so-hidden message in the older woman's voice. She was talking about the volatile male-female chemistry building between Bryn and him. A chemistry he could neutralize any time he wanted. Except for that unwanted physical arousal, he could turn off this feeling. What was bothering him had nothing personal to do with this flighty female with the expensive haircut and obvious time on her hands. Yes, she'd managed to stir up forgotten needs and touch him down deep in those dark and lonely places in less than twenty minutes, but that didn't mean a thing. Dammit to hell. He didn't want Bryn Madison. All he wanted was his bar back!

TWO

Rick never thought a surprise encounter with Liza Manning could be considered a blessing, but today that was a distinct possibility. The sixtyish widow with the steel-colored braids usually had a problem she insisted only "Captain Parrish" could solve. Right now he'd be delighted to row the indefatigable woman all the way to Havana if she requested it.

No matter how anxious he was to end this emotionally charged discussion with Bryn, he hadn't turned into a raving lunatic. He knew Liza, and to offer her blatant encouragement would be a mistake. The widow's life was dedicated to community service, along with drawing everyone she could into the same endeavor. As often as possible he managed to sidestep her efforts to involve him in her projects. True, no one cared more about Coconut Key than him, but it wasn't his style to get himself included in Liza's endless committee meetings. Not that he or anyone could escape her for long. Liza had talked him into painting the fire hall, signing a petition for an enhanced version of the recycling program, and taking the kindergarten class on a fishing trip—a trip that had cost him two good rods and an afternoon of unrelenting depression. All this in one seven-day period.

"I got back this afternoon, Liza. I just heard about Pappy," he said, moving away from Bryn. Standing in the doorway, Liza gave a sympathetic shake of her head as Rick strode by her and headed toward the bar. A bar with no beer. Balling his fists, he resisted the urge to cringe. Bryn Madison was ruining the place.

"Pappy's accident was shameful, wasn't it, Captain?" Without waiting for Rick's response, Liza went on. "Bryn visits in the morning and I get over to see him in the afternoon. We both agree that there's nothing worse than being alone in the hospital."

Liza motioned for Bryn to come into the barroom. "I know you're busy, dear, but won't you join us?"

"I . . . really shouldn't."

Without the jukebox playing or the customers' noisy chatter, he could hear clearly the hesitation in Bryn's voice. Had he been so aggressive that she was trying to avoid him? Or was she trying to get rid of him gracefully? And why the hell was he thinking about any of this? He had places to go, people to see, and a business to run. As far as Bryn Madison was concerned, she could "hesitate" her sexy body right off Coconut Key.

"Look at these, Liza." Bryn appeared in the doorway with a handful of purple cloth. "The order arrived from South Carolina a few hours ago. This screaming heliotrope isn't going to work with the pastels. They're going back as quickly as I can wrap them."

"Are you sure you want to?" Liza asked. "I think festive colors bring out the best in people," she said, touching the brim of her lemon-colored hat.

Seizing the opportunity to get away from the stew of emotions he was up to his neck in, Rick said, "Since I don't have an opinion on purple napkins, I'll leave you two to discuss their fate while I get on over to the marina."

If he hadn't been looking at Bryn, he would have been halfway to the stairs by the time he'd finished his sentence. He should have waved and left, but he made the fatal mistake of watching her a second too long. The way she crossed her arms and leaned against a doorjamb shouldn't mesmerize him, but it did. With the purple material caught in a casual crush between her arms and breasts, she'd again managed to expose that luscious few inches of flesh at her waist. From that handy spot his gaze took a slow tantalizing journey north to her unrelenting stare. Knowing her for less than an hour, he was already recognizing "the look." That confident expression daring him to say something else stupid. Before he had the chance, his view was suddenly eclipsed by Liza's ample body.

With her spine straight and her blouse puffing around her, Liza sailed into his line of vision like a magnificent ship. "Hold on, Captain Parrish, I have something to say that you'll want to hear."

Doubting that, he winced. Twice. Once at Liza's refusal to let him leave. And again at Bryn's reaction, a whispered repetition of "Captain Parrish."

He had no idea how he was going to explain the "Captain" part to her, when he didn't fully understand it himself. There were plenty of fishing-boat captains on Coconut Key, but only he had ended up with the appellation permanently attached to his name. Keeping his eyes on the older woman, he willed her to state her case so he could leave. He didn't have to wait long.

"During the Friends of the Library meeting last night," Liza said, "we started talking about the deplorable condition of our ambulance. Did you know that Pappy Madison had to be taken to the hospital in the back of Sol Bernstein's pickup truck because the gas tank on the ambulance was corroded through? The tank's been replaced, but it's only a matter of time before something else goes on it."

"Bad situation, all right," Rick said, trying to ignore the tapping of Bryn's high heels. He had to get out of there before he let himself get sucked into another conversation.

"My grandfather had to be taken to the hospital in a pickup truck?" The rat-tat-tat of her high heels filled his ears as she hurried to the bar, her hands pressed flat against her collarbone. "No one told me that."

"Yes, dear, I'm afraid that's what happened. With the ambulance in that condition, the medical emergency team couldn't get over here to Pappy any faster than Sol and Tweed MacNeil could load him up and take him. They did the best they could, but Pappy was hurting something awful by the time they got him to the emergency room." The older woman pulled on her braids and looked at the floor. "Captain Parrish can tell you how important good ambulance service can be, because—"

"Liza," he said, cutting her off, "what did you have to tell me?" He meant for his hard stare to be a warning to the older woman. He knew his attempt to silence her on that personal and painful subject had worked when her lips formed an even line and her gaze dropped to the floor again. That's all he needed, bringing Angie into it. Both he and Liza turned their embarrassed faces toward Bryn.

By the horrified look in her eyes, he knew Bryn was still picturing her grandfather in the back of the truck. Rick recognized the prolonged reaction and, without stopping to think of the repercussions, reached out to give her a reassuring touch. His thumb grazed her skin, and before he thought it through, he was giving her shoulder a comforting rub.

"Hey, everything's okay now," he said softly. "You told me the doctor said he's going to be fine."

"I know," she said, staring out at the palm fronds brushing against the rail, "but it hurts to picture him like that. Waiting for help, then bouncing around in the back of a truck. No trained medical people to help him."

For one earth-stopping moment, Rick was jolted back to an afternoon five years ago. The sequence of events flashed through his mind, leaving him with the raw taste of his remembered fear. He squeezed his eyes shut in a private moment of hell. Dammit, how many times would he have to relive that afternoon? Forcing himself to focus on Bryn, he began squeezing her shoulder. "People do the best they can."

"That's right, Captain Parrish," Liza said. "And that's what I have a mind to do."

Brought back to his senses by Liza's no-nonsense tone, Rick lifted his fingers from Bryn's shoulder. As casually as he could, he stepped back and slid both his hands into his pockets. Everyone experienced tragedy, but that didn't call for a group hug. What was he thinking of, touching her like that? He'd survived the last five years without succumbing to smarmy displays of emotion. "Let's hear it, Liza," he said brusquely.

"I want to have a community fund-raiser to buy a new ambulance for Coconut Key."

"Why not put it to a referendum? Next county election is—"

"Too long to wait," said Liza, interrupting with

a waving index finger. "I need you to advertise it at your marina. And I'll need Bryn's help too."

"You want me?" Bryn's head came up, her eyes meeting first with Liza's and then with Rick's. Pressing both hands to her midriff, she asked, "But what could I do?"

"That's what everyone asks," Liza said, dipping her chin to look over her glasses and smile. "You're a breath of fresh air, and that's enough to start with. But more importantly, you're motivated to help because of what's happened to Pappy." She patted Rick's arm. "How about a little encouragement, Captain?"

"How long are you planning to stay?" he asked. No matter what message his body was sending him, he was not interested in the way she was touching herself. There was simply nothing else to look at.

"I'm not certain." Bryn looked around the room. "It depends on a lot of things."

Keeping his gaze on Bryn, he said, "Well, Liza, she tells me she cares about Coconut Key, but if she's not going to be around long enough to—"

"I'll be around," she said, swiveling her head in his direction.

"Really?" he asked, shifting his weight as he gave her his cockiest smile.

"Really."

Studying her for the first signs of fidgeting, he finally turned his attention to Liza and shrugged. "Then sure, I'll give her my vote."

"I'll be glad to sell tickets and even advertise once the restaurant is opened, but I don't have any experience with planning a fund-raiser. As you both can see, I'm putting together this restaurant and looking after my grandfather's affairs. Then there's my own business I'm keeping tabs on. I don't think I'll have the time for much else."

Liza laughed a self-satisfied laugh. "Everyone is reluctant to get involved, but once you're working on the planning committee, I know you'll do Pappy proud as you always do. He's told me you've worked with subcontractors and cranky clients. Considering your successful business, it's obvious you have the organizational skills. Coupled with your charm, I don't see any problems."

Pretending to scan the paint job on the wall behind her, Rick wasn't missing a blink in Bryn's worried expression. Was she thinking of a way to stay off the committee or a way to get on it?

"Charity committees are different, Liza. I'd be working with nonprofessionals." She shook her head. "I really don't think I ought to get involved."

Smiling at Rick, the older woman wiggled her index finger. "Is this the same young woman who, minutes ago, was shouting something about how much she cared for Coconut Key and its people?"

"Well, yes—" Bryn began, tugging at the strands of hair falling onto her forehead.

"And the same young woman gasping from the

image of her grandfather being transported to the hospital in the back of a pickup truck?"

Bryn nodded.

Liza threw up her hands. "Then I know I can count on you to do a great job heading the committee."

"*Heading* the committee? Oh, Liza, I just can't see how I could handle that along with everything else."

Rick pressed his lips together to suppress the snicker he knew was coming. Watching Bryn trying to politely sidestep the older woman's request was giving him tremendous satisfaction. But it was short-lived and hollow once he realized that he'd sized up Bryn perfectly after all. Although she was concerned about her grandfather, she was like so many other outsiders. She would stick around long enough to stir things up, then she would head on out the moment her restaurant experiment failed. The important issues, like the need for a new ambulance, paled next to her cloth party hats and lace valances. Her shallowness set his teeth on edge. Where was her Mary Sunshine demeanor now?

"Everyone talks about helping, but when it's time to do something," Liza said, her words beginning to echo Rick's opinion of Bryn. "I don't know . . ." Her voice trailed off in tones of well-practiced, sympathy-provoking despair.

Having exhausted all her reasons for not heading the committee, Bryn slid her gaze toward Rick.

She couldn't figure out what was more upsetting, his smug I-told-you-so smile or her growing guilt about attempting to talk her way out of the committee. Darn him. It was none of Rick Parrish's concern that she was exploring the possibility of moving her business and herself to the Keys. Because of her extended visit, she was learning about the business climate there. A number of places needed design services, and there had to be dozens more she hadn't yet discovered. Since her established clients were scattered across the country, she could base her operation anywhere. And there were other incentives for moving that she couldn't ignore. Truth was, those unfinished issues between her and her grandfather kept tugging at her heart now that she was near him. But Rick Parrish didn't need to know any of that. What he needed was to wipe that supercilious expression from his face. And she wanted to be the one to do it for him. The more she looked at Rick, the more she felt challenged to immediate action.

"Forgive me, Liza. You're right," Bryn said, nodding. "Too many people talk about how they care for their community, but when it comes to the hard work, most aren't there for it. Rick agrees with me. Passionately."

"That's true," he said, staring hard at her. "A person could drown with the rush of soapbox sentiments flooding this place."

"Right again . . . Captain," Bryn said, wrapping her

voice in innocent enthusiasm. While he had been busily restating his opinion of her, she was happily sharpening her own barbed comeback. "Everything you said in the kitchen makes perfect sense. People should get involved more. I'd be honored to head the committee."

Liza's hands went to her hips. "Now, that's simply wonderf—"

"Under one condition," she quickly added.

Liza's sparkling smile of victory dimmed, her eyelids blinking beneath the flipped-up brim of her hat. "And what would that one condition be, dear?"

"I'm going to need a cochairman," she said, clasping her hands behind her. Stepping past both of them, Bryn turned to lean her shoulder against a support column. Pausing for effect, she waited until she had their total, albeit wary attention. "Let's see. It'll have to be someone who knows the people here. Knows how to inspire others. A person who not only says he cares, but who'll be willing to prove it with involvement every step of the way."

"What about that, Liza?" Rick asked, looking decidedly uneasy. "Can you think of anyone?"

Raising her eyebrows, Liza opened her mouth. "Well—"

"Don't bother, Liza," she said, pushing off the column to take a step toward Rick. "I've already thought of someone."

"Really, dear? Who?"

Bryn looked up at Rick, raising her eyebrows slowly. A second later Liza whispered an "Oooooh," followed by her own list of reasons why Rick was the obvious and only choice for the job.

Rick wasn't listening to a word the older woman said. He appeared to be concentrating all his efforts on not wringing Bryn's neck. But Bryn knew by his intrusive gaze that although he'd like to, he wasn't going to fight her on this. How could he after that explosive speech he'd given her minutes ago?

"So you'll do it, Captain Parrish? You'll cochair the committee with Bryn?"

"How could I say no?" he asked, slowly shifting his gaze to Liza.

"Yes. How could you?" Bryn countered, enhancing the sweetness of her tone with a casual shrug. Stepping back, she allowed Rick plenty of space to maneuver around them.

"Ladies," he said, pulling his sunglasses from his pocket and slipping them on. "I'm sure you'll get back to me on this."

"We will," they said together.

The older woman moved to the north rail as Bryn watched him head for the stairs. When he disappeared down them, she continued staring at where he'd been. "What have I gotten myself into, Liza?"

"I assume you're referring more to working with Captain Parrish than to taking charge of the committee."

"That's it exactly," she said, dragging her hand along the bar as she turned to face Liza. "Oh, look, he forgot to take his jacket." Grabbing it off the bar, she said, "I'll run it down to him—" She broke off as Liza, shaking her head, crooked a finger.

"Not just yet, dear."

She joined Liza, looking over the rail to where the older woman was pointing. As if on cue, Rick appeared below them.

Holding his jacket in her arms, Bryn studied the enigmatic man as he made his way through the palm grove toward his marina. If he'd been anyone else, she would have wished that this view of him were her last. But he wasn't like anyone else she'd ever met. He made her defensive about things she'd never felt defensive about before. He made her angry, too, and he also made her wonder how he accomplished those things. The strangest thing of all was that he made her want to get closer to him, to understand why all that passion sizzled inside him and what it would be like to unleash it . . . with her.

"It's going to be lovely having such an intelligent woman in charge of this committee," Liza said as she left the railing and started across the room toward the stairs.

Bryn wasn't through looking at the broad-shouldered man strolling across the hard-packed sand. He'd shoved both hands into his trouser pockets and picked up his pace, making the material pull snug against his backside. Her face warmed with feminine appreciation. "But, Liza," she said, turning her face and then her eyes to the older woman, "Rick is cochairing this committee with me."

Liza took her broad-brimmed straw hat from her head. Feeding the curved edge through her fingers, she smiled to herself before looking at Bryn. "Like I said, it's going to be lovely having an intelligent woman in charge of the committee." Plopping the hat back on her head, she tipped it sideways before continuing toward the stairs.

"But—" Bryn said, trying to gather her thoughts for a believable protest. That task was impossible with her attention bouncing back and forth between Liza's jaunty steps and Rick's enticing body.

"Don't be in such a hurry to get the jacket back to him. He'll be along for it one of these days. And don't worry about the committee work either. I'll bring the necessary paperwork to your first meeting. Let me know when you want to hold it." Liza kept on walking, finally turning around when she neared the stairs. "I'm on my way over to the hospital. I'll tell Pappy what you've done. He'll be so proud of you. And Bryn?"

"Yes?"

"You're not going to be sorry you took this on."

"It's because of Pappy that I'm—"

"Oh, I understand perfectly, dear. I'm nearly seventy, you know." She gave Bryn a slow, soft wink before turning the corner. "Enjoy."

Bryn felt a quirky smile forming. Drawing her fingertips across her lips, she looked back over the rail. There was no use arguing. She'd hardly taken her eyes off Rick since the moment she first saw him. His energy had been flying around her like a bottle rocket, and capturing him for the committee was the most exhilarating thing Bryn had done all day. His vital presence was still affecting her, and to deny that would be lying to herself. Besides, from this distance she *was* still enjoying her view of him. If Liza got a kick out of that, no one was getting hurt.

For a few seconds she lost sight of him among the dozen or so people milling around the dock. It wasn't as if he'd fallen into the water and drowned, but she couldn't tell that by the way her heart fluttered in her chest, then jumped when she spotted him by the bait shack.

One of his employees was handing him a clipboard. She couldn't hear their conversation, but the way the men were crowding around him and reaching to shake his hand strongly indicated that Rick Parrish fit his title well. "Captain," she whispered to herself. Commanding. Respected. And most intriguing of all, alone among his men. Gripping the rail, she strained to keep him in sight, then scolded herself for the action. Allowing one brief encounter with a man to affect her this way wasn't like her. No, not like her at all, she told herself, hanging over the rail for another indulgent glance. And connecting with a stubborn, self-possessed male was the last thing she needed. Getting involved in a new work project was where her focus should be, not feeding her curiosity about an opinionated man. Still, there was passion beneath the slightly weathered skin of the handsome fishing-boat captain. Hidden passion that was fighting for expression. By his steely reaction to its unbidden display, she knew he worked hard to keep it hidden, as carefully hidden as she kept hers.

But this afternoon, in a glorious explosion of emotion, he'd failed. She was still feeling aftershocks when she pictured the way he'd met her stare. She wanted to laugh off the phenomenon, but not as much as she wanted it repeated. Pushing up from the rail, she stopped before she turned around. Indulging herself in one more sensual tremor wouldn't be the end of the world. She strained her chin in the direction of the marina. To her surprise Rick raised his head and met her eyes. From forty yards away she sensed him daring her to look away first. "After you, Captain Parrish," she whispered. Then someone jostled him and their moment ended, but like a forbidden kiss, it left her wanting more.

The following morning Rick made his way down the hospital corridor toward Pappy's room. Trying to escape the antiseptic smell, he held his breath and quickened his pace. By the time he reached Pappy's door, his stomach was churning and his mind was filling with images of Angie. Pushing open the door, he threw his energy into a blustery greeting.

"For crissakes, Pappy, I told you something like this was going to happen if you kept chasing the ladies. Which one did it? The blond gift shop owner over on the highway or one of the Fagan twins?"

"About time you got over here," Pappy said, ignoring Rick's questions while keeping the mock gruffness going between them. "I could have died and been desiccated by now."

"Desiccated, Pappy? Has someone been sneaking you the *New York Times* crossword puzzle again?"

"Yes, someone has," came a familiar voice from behind the privacy curtain. He heard the click of a light switch and then her footsteps. "Hello, Captain Parrish." Bryn brushed by him to settle a vase of yellow carnations on Pappy's nightstand. While she fluffed the ferns and adjusted the ribbon, he remembered what Liza had said. *"Bryn visits in the morning."*

He also remembered deciding not to stare at her again. After locking gazes with her across the palm grove yesterday, he came to a few other conclusions too.

Plain and simple, he wanted her stretched across his bed, feathering her fingertips between her breasts, lowering those curly lashes at him and whispering shameless suggestions. But he'd be damned if he'd ever let things go that far. He wasn't looking for a complicated relationship. And she was just the type to make it complicated. Besides, no matter what Bryn Madison said, she would soon be gone from Coconut Key.

"Hello, Bryn." He hooked his thumbs in his waistband and held on tightly when she turned to smile at him. No, it was definitely not safe to look too long at those amber eyes. And looking at the rest of her wasn't safe either. Her blue-and-white-striped top was coming dangerously close to slipping off her shoulder. That sun-kissed shoulder, all rosy and sprinkled with freckles, was making his mouth water. He moved his gaze out of one danger zone and into another. Lord help him for thinking it, but he could forget about those blue bicycle shorts ever slipping off as easily as her top. Those shorts would have to be peeled off with both hands and a groan. He cleared his throat. "Sorry I interrupted your visit." Turning on his heel, he headed for the door. "I'll come back later."

"That's okay," she said, following him. "You stay. I'll go out for a while."

"I insist," he said, reaching for the handle and bumping her hand in the process. Her cool touch sent prickles spiraling up his fingers and over his hand. Taking an extra breath, he pulled in her scent along with it. That cool cream and cinnamony scent. He wanted to breathe it in again. Moving in closer, he reassured himself that the pleasure of her fragrance was nothing more than a welcomed respite from the antiseptic odors.

"No, really. This is your first visit with him since you—"

"What are you two talking about? There are four chairs and an extra bed in this room. Get back here, the both of you," Pappy said.

Laughing, Bryn let go of the handle and walked back to the bed. "I'm told his grouchiness is a sign he's getting better."

Rick studied her relaxed posture and the teasing look she gave Pappy. So this was how she was going to play it. As if her decision to run out of the room were based on politeness and not an attempt to escape him. He looked at her again as she reached for a chocolate on the bedside table. Taking a bite, she sighed loudly and sat down. "I love dark chocolate. Would you like a piece, Rick?"

He'd love a piece all right, but he wasn't thinking about candy. Rolling his eyes, he quietly cursed himself for the roguish thought. She hadn't been trying to escape him. She *was* relaxed. He was the one with the sweaty palms and lusty thoughts. "No thanks," he said, walking around to the other side of the bed. Taking a chair, he spun it around, pushed it closer to the bed, and straddled it. "So, Pappy, how are they treating you?"

"Terrible. They stapled my bone together, took away my cigars, and stuck me in a room without cable

TV. There's nothing to do. And just to torture me," he added, stabbing the air with his finger, "they have me peeing in a bottle."

"They did not staple your bone, Grandfather, they inserted a pin."

"I'm bored out of my skull."

"Really? Your nurses tell me you spend half your day playing poker with the housekeeping staff. They can't get anything done."

Pappy stared at the ceiling and pursed his lips. "Maybe it's not all that bad being stuck in here. At least I haven't been shanghaied onto one of Liza's committees."

"Captain Parrish wasn't shanghaied," Bryn said, scolding her grandfather with a wave of her hand. "He didn't even put up a fuss when I asked him to cochair it with me. Right, Captain?" She nibbled the corner from another piece of candy.

There she goes again, he thought, smiling so sweetly it made his teeth ache. Well, he'd be damned if he'd allow her smile to get to him, especially when she was shining it on Pappy. If she would stop nibbling chocolates with those pearly white teeth and give him more than a passing glance, she would know he was a changed man. A man dedicated to redefining stoicism; Bryn Madison was not going to rattle his chain again.

He waited.

And waited.

She kept her attention on Pappy, feeding him chocolates while bantering with him about pretty nurses and the perils of cheating at poker. Shifting in his chair, Rick shoved his fingers through his hair. Like an uncontrollable current, her laughter moved through him, tangling his serious mood with unasked-for pleasure. Each time she brushed back her hair, or dropped her chin on the backs of her fingers, or brought a piece of chocolate to her mouth, he felt a tug down low in his gut. Dammit, he hadn't come here to watch her lick caramel from her lips. "Pappy, has Bryn been filling you in on her changes at the Crab Shack?"

The old man's eyes brightened. "No, but I'm sure she's doing a bang-up job. She knows all about these things. She's got her own interior design business." He beamed at his granddaughter. "You redid that room of the real estate mogul in New York, didn't you, Brynnie? It was in a magazine."

"I did," she said. "Three times. Remember me telling you about how he and his wife kept changing their minds?" she said, laughing with the memory. "They finally settled on the English garden look because she said she wanted to feel comfortable serving tea cakes and cucumber sandwiches."

Terrific. She'd dealt with people from a different universe. He dropped his chin on his forearms. "This could be worse than I thought," he mumbled to himself.

"Excuse me?" she said, blinking with surprise.

"You know what I'm talking about, Bryn. The people who come to the Crab Shack aren't interested in tea cakes or cucumber sandwiches. And unless they can squirt them from plastic packets, French sauces are out too."

Pushing away from the bed rail, she straightened her back. "Well I'm not a complete idiot when it comes to understanding clientele."

Standing up, he spoke directly to Pappy. "Don't get me wrong. I'm sure whatever she did up North was successful there, but we are talking about Coconut Key. I think you're in danger of losing your shirt over this."

With his eyebrows raised, Pappy's gaze flicked from one visitor to the other.

"Don't listen to him, Grandfather," Bryn said, standing as she patted the old man's arm. "Everything's coming along beautifully."

"You haven't opened yet," Rick reminded her loudly.

Grabbing the bed rail, she leaned over Pappy and matched Rick's volume. "But when I do, the people of Coconut Key are going to love having a well-appointed restaurant."

Rick met her halfway across the bed. "That's your opinion, and unfortunately for Pappy, it happens to be wrong."

"May I remind you that my opinion," she asked, pressing her fingers between her breasts, "happens to be valued by some people?"

"And may I remind you, again, that Pappy hasn't seen the changes yet?"

She was about to respond when the door swung open behind her. A nurse rushed in waving a blood pressure cuff.

"That's quite enough. We can hear you at the nurses' station." She pointed over her shoulder. "Out, you two! Right now."

"Aw, jeez, Ruthie! Don't send them out," Pappy said. "This is getting interesting."

"That's all right, Grandfather," Bryn said, leaning down to drop a kiss on Pappy's brow. "I'll be back once I've explained a few things to Captain Parrish." Without looking in Rick's direction, she breezed out of the room.

"Sorry, Pappy." Rick swore under his breath as he headed around the bed for the door. Yanking it open, he went out after her into the hall. She wasn't there.

He found her standing a few yards away in the middle of a pale blue alcove, her hands primly folded near the juncture of her thighs and her eyes fixed straight ahead. Except for that exposed shoulder, she was a living shrine to dignity. Unfortunately, he wasn't in the mood for a religious experience.

Several charged seconds ticked by as he tried to keep his eyes off her temptingly displayed flesh. The graceful angularity of her shoulder was hard to ignore. The more he stared, the more it seemed to beg for his touch. Clearing his throat, he shifted his weight from one leg to the other. "Think we raised his blood pressure?"

"Probably, since mine is about to go through the roof," she said, staring at the fire extinguisher hanging on the opposite wall.

The silence returned, broken by an occasional ringing telephone and soft, distant laughter. He rubbed the back of his neck and wondered if he should sit down and be quiet. He started for a chair, then stopped beside her. The hell he'd be quiet. He would give her one last chance, and if she didn't want to listen, he would can the effort to communicate with her. Permanently.

Forcing his voice low, he turned to her. "Look, Bryn, I still think I'm on track about the new restaurant. Even if you won't face facts, Pappy has the right to hear another opinion."

Crossing her arms in front of her, she tapped her shiny red fingernails against her forearms before turning her wide-eyed gaze in his direction. She studied him as she licked the corner of her mouth thoughtfully. "You are right about one thing."

Yesss! Triumph at last. She'd come to her senses; there was justice in the world. Well, whatever it was that she was about to tell him, he would accept it stoically. He lowered his chin, hoping she'd interpret the gesture as an invitation to begin. While he waited, he fought back the urge to gather her into his arms and track down the source of her scent. In the morning, after her shower, where *did* she dab it? He pictured himself starting the search at the high hollow of her shoulder, then nuzzling her all the way to that place between her breasts . . . and maybe lower. As if she'd read his thoughts, Bryn's lips parted with a tiny gasp. *Share with me, Bryn. What are you thinking while I'm making love to you in my mind?* He began lowering his head. She was tilting her face up to meet his. The closer he came, the sweeter her lips looked. At the moment Rick sensed their tickling touch, a jolting voice called out to them from down the hall.

"If you two can control yourselves, you can go back into him. One at a time."

He pulled up first. "Go on in. I'll come back later," he said, as reality crashed between them. She started away from him, but he reached out to stop her. "Before you go, I'm still curious."

"About what?" she asked, looking slightly shaken by what had almost happened.

"What is that one thing you think I'm right about?"

She hesitated, then pressed her fingertips against the front of his shirt and looked up at him through her thick lashes. For one pulse of a moment he thought she was going to kiss him. Really kiss him. His hands itched to hold her close and help her make it a long, wet one.

But he wanted more than a kiss. He wanted to bury himself in the tantalizing puzzle she was to him.

"Oh, yes," she whispered as if she'd just remembered. "You were right when you said that whatever he does with his restaurant is none of your business." Stepping away from him, she adjusted her striped top, then started back down the hall toward Pappy's room.

Watching her go with her little victory riding high on her shoulders, he couldn't help but smile. She'd pulled out of the charged moment neatly, earning the right to strut. This time. Nodding, he allowed himself to enjoy her deliciously sexy gait while he thought about the coming weeks.

In winning this skirmish, she had also gifted him with a challenge, and he never backed down from a challenge. Especially when it involved Pappy's Crab Shack, and in a larger sense the preservation of Coconut Key. But with her unique blend of feminine subtleties and fiery passion, he wondered how he was going to go about fighting for his own preservation.

THREE

"What are you waiting for, dear?"

Before Bryn could answer, Liza continued speaking, her voice as urgent over the telephone as it was in person.

With the receiver tucked snugly between her shoulder and ear, Bryn packed the last box lunch into the carton, then sank into the old pine captain's chair next to the wall phone. There was something oddly comforting about the worn armrests and the firm curve supporting her back. She'd assured herself that Rick's use of it the other day had nothing to do with why she'd chosen to drag this particular chair into Chez Madison's kitchen. Entwining the coiled phone cord through her fingers, she smoothed a tight fist along the hem of her nylon running shorts when thoughts of Rick and that almost kiss slipped unbidden into her thoughts.

"Bryn dear, are you there?"

"Yes. Sorry. What were you—" she began, then broke off when she heard Liza's strangled sigh.

"We don't have a lot of time to waste, you know. Jacaranda Key is planning a water festival for next month. Islamorada and Conch Key have already started advertising for their fishing tournaments. We must lock in a date for our fund-raising activity. I'll contact your volunteers and tell them to be at the restaurant tonight."

Bryn had given a wide berth to Liza's zealous style, but tonight simply wasn't a good night to have the meeting. Furniture samples were being delivered to Chez Madison today. Before they arrived, she had her grandfather to visit and at least four calls to make concerning her design business. Once Jiggy picked up the box lunches and her morning jog was out of the way, she was going to be busy well into the night. "Liza, it's a mess over here."

"No one's going to care. All your committee people require are a few snacks and a place to eat them. By the way, Captain Parrish loves key lime pie, so keep that in mind when you're preparing the food. And since you're right next to his marina, I'll let you tell Captain Parrish to be there at eight-thirty. I'll take care of notifying the rest of the committee, and I'll drop off the folders to you later today too."

While Liza chattered on, Bryn looked across the kitchen where Rick's blazer was hanging. The navy blue linen blend was beginning to look as if it belonged in the kitchen. Even though she knew the act was a silly tactile indulgence, she caught herself touching the buttons and patting the pockets several times a day. *If you'd kissed me, Rick Parrish, I wouldn't still be wondering, waiting, wanting. . . .* If he'd kissed her, maybe she wouldn't have this overwhelming desire to keep touching his jacket. All the errant, erotic thoughts she'd been having would most likely disappear with a real flesh-on-flesh experience. She felt her mouth squinching into a self-deprecating frown. How could she have spent the last few days letting her imagination build an almost kiss into the erotic event of her life? He was probably a lousy kisser anyway. She rubbed her thumbnail back and forth across her lips. Probably a brusque kisser, hard and tight-lipped and unsatisfying. Staring at his jacket, she started to think how she could remedy the problem when Liza's voice startled her.

"Bryn, are you still there?"

"Yes," she said, getting to her feet and turning away from the jacket. *Fool*, she thought to herself, *let Rick Parrish remedy his own kissing problems. If he has any*. "I'm still here."

"Bryn?" Liza's voice was strangely soft.

"What is it?"

"Contacting Captain Parrish about the meeting isn't bothering you, is it?"

"Why do you ask?"

"I have an instinct for these things." Before Bryn could ask what "these things" were, Liza continued. "Maybe I'm out of bounds on this, but I think you ought to know how Captain Parrish's marriage ended."

"Liza, wait." A sudden and overwhelming impulse told her not to listen. Staring at her white-knuckled hands squeezing the phone, she willed herself to relax her grip. "I-I think Rick should be the one to tell me about his past." She rolled her eyes. Why, oh, why had she responded that way? When was Rick Parrish ever going to be close enough to her to tell her anything about himself, especially about a divorce? "I mean, I like to stay clear of anything resembling gossip." Great! Now she sounded like a snob.

"It's not gossip, Bryn. But you're probably right. Maybe Rick ought to tell you about it himself."

Grateful that Liza's tone was reflective, and not hurt, she said, "Yes, well, I'll go over now and talk to him." She quickly added, "About the committee meeting, I mean."

"Of course, dear."

Rick was talking quietly into the phone and didn't notice her when she walked into the marina office. Dressed in her running clothes, she stood inside the door with his jacket folded over one arm and the carton of lunches resting on her hip. Setting the carton on a display cabinet inside the door, she caught the jacket as it began slipping from her arm. Stroking it one last time, she was alarmed to realize that she was going to miss it hanging on the kitchen door. Running her fingers over the raised anchors on the brass buttons, she checked to make sure Rick wasn't looking at her before she sniffed the collar. How had a simple navy blue blazer become an object of fetish? Her search for the answer was interrupted by Rick's voice.

"I know we should have talked about it before this," he was saying, his upward gaze dropping in defeat, then wandering across the room to Bryn. Holding her gaze boldly with his own, he kept on talking into the phone, "I have to go. Sure, I'll remember. We'll talk later."

As he eased the receiver into its cradle, Bryn felt her moxie waning. Feminine instinct struggled against common sense. Was his phone conversation about an upcoming fishing charter or a date? And why should it matter? While she'd been mooning over him for days, he had been avoiding her.

"Good morning," he said, before pointing to her red running clothes. "Challenging me to a race this morning?"

"Hello. What?" Looking down at her clothes, she said, "No," before brushing back her hair. A bouncy lock dipped across her brow again, but this time she pretended to ignore it. What had possessed her to give up hair spray and extra-body styling gel since she'd been down here? "I didn't mean to disturb your phone call."

"You didn't. I was through," he said, picking up a pencil and writing on a clipboard. He looked up at her long enough to register the point with a smile. Turning back to the clipboard, he erased what he'd written, then wrote again.

So it wasn't a lover he'd been talking with. Her shoulders relaxed along with her tightly clamped jaw. The call must have been about a charter, because he continued to write down numbers in little squares and make check marks in several columns. Standing by the display of potato chips and cheese curls, she had a nearly overwhelming urge to tear open the cellophane and toss them into the air like confetti.

"So, what's up?" he asked, hanging the clipboard on a wall hook and sliding the pencil onto the counter beside the cash register.

"Jiggy doesn't have to pick up the lunches. I brought them myself," she said, indicating the carton on the display cabinet. "Two roast beefs, three chicken salads, and one peanut butter and jelly. I put in extra pickles and pasta salad. And French apple pie. I didn't have any key lime." Why was she reciting the menu? He hadn't asked.

"Jiggy's coming by to see you later. He's bringing Miss Scarlett back to Pappy's." Rick shook his head, fighting back a laugh as he rolled his tongue inside his cheek.

"What's wrong?"

"Jiggy's love life. Seems the parrot starts spouting scripture at the worst possible moment, and by the time he quiets the bird . . ."

"I see," she said, exaggerating her nod. If anyone but Rick had told her, she would have been laughing out loud, but instead all she felt was a stinging rush of blood to her face. Why did she let him get to her like this? she wondered angrily. Swallowing, she took a step forward and began again. "You forgot your jacket."

He was pouring himself a cup of coffee. "I thought I might have left it at Pappy's," he said, twisting to look at her while he squeezed honey onto a spoon. "Would you like a cup?"

"No, thank you." Why hadn't he come by for the jacket if he thought he left it there? Why hadn't he at least called about it? Why hadn't he . . . ? The silent questions building in her head suddenly exploded. "Why haven't you answered the messages I left on your answering machine?" she demanded. He *hadn't* been answering her phone calls for a full five days, but that was no reason to blurt it out like a recalcitrant teenager.

The air conditioner started in with a warning rattle and then a blast of frigid air.

"Sorry about that," he said evenly. "I've had a lot of unfinished business to deal with since I got back from my trip."

Giving his coffee one last stir, he clinked the spoon

against the edge of the mug before lifting it to his mouth. He did a thorough job of licking the residue of honey from the inside curve of the spoon and then the outside curve. The action was an everyday one, ordinary and commonplace, but when Rick performed it, it vibrated with erotic overtones. Suddenly she was picturing him sliding his tongue over her curves. Her eyes began closing.

"You're right," he said as he dropped the spoon onto the tray with a loud clatter. "I should have called you back before now. I apologize."

She searched his guileless expression, trying to find a sign that he knew what he'd been doing to her, but her gaze kept coming back to the shine on his lips. She could almost smell the warm honey and, if she leaned closer, taste it. She wondered what he'd do if she ran her tongue over his lips. Encourage further exploration? Images of their naked bodies tangled together filled her mind until she had to pull in a long and calming lungful of air. Why was she allowing these images to continue? Eroticism had been a much-heralded but ultimately disappointing undertaking for her. Still, she couldn't seem to stop thinking about what being with him would be like. Attempting to banish the confusing thoughts and the accompanying tension they produced, she tilted her head to a comical angle. "Yes, you should have called me . . . but I have you here now."

"Yes, you do," he said, reaching back with his hands

and lifting himself onto the counter. "Up against the wall, as a matter of fact." Picking up his mug, he examined its sailfish decal before rubbing his knuckles over it. Before she could yell "Stop!" he was licking drops of honey from his fingers. "Hot," he murmured before looking up at her. "So what are you going to do with me?"

She'd stared a moment too long at his fingers. His incredibly sexy, wet fingers. Down went her guard in a rush of delicious confusion. What was he saying?

Hot?

Wet?

Up against the wall?

What was *she* going to do with *him*?

Streaming heat pooled in forgotten places inside her. Her lips felt full and tingling. For one lost second she felt like doing something very foolish. Very sexy. Very unlike herself. Finding herself in a free fall through her wildest fantasies, she struggled against them. He kept on smiling. Kept on staring. Kept on melting her resolve to pull out of this vortex of sensuality. And he was winning. Her hand drifted across her midriff before languidly moving to her arm. "Our first committee meeting is tonight. . . ." She traced a long line down her arm, paused at her wrist, then dragged her fingertips up to her elbow. Perhaps it was the way his stare locked onto her movements, but her voice was beginning to sound low and sultry even to herself.

"Tonight," he repeated, his voice dropping into a whisper suggestive of murmured endearments and soft kisses.

Somewhere in all of this pseudo-foreplay she had to pull out and land on her feet. And soon. But not too soon. She took an extra breath before sending him the beginning of an invitation with a tiny lick of her lips. Holding his jacket against her hip, she moved forward and placed one hand on the counter. "They're all coming to Chez Madison at eight-thirty, but if you wanted to—"

"Tonight?" The teasing maze of moves he'd been guiding her through went straight out the window with his bitten-off curse and shifting gaze. "I have something on my schedule for tonight."

Don't stop this, she wanted to tell him. Don't stop this fresh energy tickling at my heart. I like it. I like the way it feels. Please don't do this because I called it Chez Madison instead of Pappy's Crab Shack. Please don't make me say anything reckless. Blood was pounding in her ears from sheer embarrassment, but that didn't keep her from whispering, "I need you there, Rick. Couldn't you ask someone else to help you out?"

With an almost apologetic tone, he shook his head. "I can't get out of this, Bryn. Look, if I can make it later, I'll come by. Or maybe you could reschedule."

Reschedule? Instead of a lovers' rendezvous, he made it sound like a business meeting. Her heart skipped a beat and she almost groaned out loud; it *was* a business meeting. Her hand dropped to her side as the sensual fog burned away, leaving her in a room filled with fishing tackle, sunscreen, and brightly colored hats that read Fish or Cut Bait.

"Maybe you could reschedule," she said smartly, brushing her hair from her brow. She waited in silence until she felt her ears smarting with his answer.

"I can't."

Lifting her hand from the glass counter top, she straightened her spine. "The meeting's at eight-thirty," she said, clinging to the cool professionalism she willed to return to her voice. She headed for the door, but before her hand closed around the doorknob, more words welled up from a raw spot inside her. She could barely contain the hot anger she felt. "I'm busy too. I'm trying to run my business by phone from down here. I'm up to my neck in renovations at the restaurant. And my grandfather needs me." Twisting the knob, she fumbled twice before yanking open the door. "I don't have time to chase down the rest of the committee to reschedule this for your convenience, Captain Parrish."

She didn't mean to rattle the glass panes in the door when she pulled it shut, but when she returned a second later to place the jacket on his counter, she didn't apologize. If she did that, he might turn his face from the window and see the stinging tears in her eyes. Then he'd ask why they were there, and she wasn't sure she knew the answer.

⊰⊱————————————————⊰⊱

He hadn't lied to Bryn; he couldn't get out of his plans. He'd put them off too long as it was. Facing Sharon Burke and telling her their arrangement had to end wasn't going to be easy. For the next hour he busied himself with paperwork while he waited for his customers. Several times he stopped, pencil poised in midair, while he tried to think of a way to let Sharon down easily. Thumbing through one of his astronomy magazines hadn't helped either. In the end he decided to rely on the one thing Sharon always insisted on. Honesty.

Picking up Bryn's carton of lunches, he walked out to the *Coral Kiss*. Below deck, he lifted out the first box to place in the cooler. She'd wrapped each one in banana-yellow ribbon with a hand-lettered card attached. He tipped the card to read it. *Chez Madison—distinctive cuisine near the heart of the Keys*. Shaking his head, he laughed softly. If he didn't admire her goal, he had to admire her perseverance. After storing the food, he went topside hoping to catch a glimpse of her upstairs at Pappy's in the open-air room. He never got the chance to look for her, because his group charter was climbing out of their van in the parking lot. As they gathered their gear he jumped down onto the dock and directed them inside the office to sign several forms. While he waited, he found himself thinking about the woman he would see tonight. Maybe with him out of her life, she could start thinking about a plan for the rest of it. About goals. And about finding the courage to move on.

Sharon Burke was a good person, and after her husband died, a lonely one like himself. There were plenty of men lined up to impress the lovely widow, but as she told him, no one understood that she wasn't looking for another husband. Just a decent man to talk to, a man who didn't demand her constant attention when she simply wasn't ready to give it.

At first, talking was all they'd both wanted. All they needed. Their no-strings relationship hadn't slipped mindlessly into a sexual one. They'd rationalized that move two years ago. When the need to find comfort and release grew strong enough, one of them would make a phone call to the other. Since she had been the last one to call over two months ago, he knew it was his turn. Maybe it was because of his visit to Angie's parents, but he kept putting off calling Sharon. Like a habit, his relationship with Sharon demanded little attention, required minimum imagination, and offered no challenge. His life had drifted on. Then Bryn with her peekaboo clothes, disturbing ways, and determined attitude blew into his life like an unannounced hurricane. No matter how hard he tried to discount his attraction to Pappy's grand-daughter, he'd known from the moment he'd met Bryn that it was time to end his relationship with Sharon.

As he directed his customers aboard the *Coral Kiss*, he felt a sense of relief along with impatience to get the day over with, and to get on with his plans for tonight. Glancing out at the open water beyond the marina, he repositioned his ball cap and asked loudly, "Anyone here fish these waters before?" Through a chorus of noes, Rick came back with, "Aw, hell, neither have I." Everyone laughed, and as they motored out of the slip, he had the feeling that his attempt at humor had more to do with relaxing himself than his customers.

The rest of the day Bryn worked on turning Pappy's Crab Shack into Chez Madison. As she watched the sample furniture being carried upstairs, she realized a moment of sweet triumph. Rick was going to hate the pastel upholstery and the delicate flowers carved into the light wood. Positioning the chairs around the tables, she told herself it would serve him right to cringe every time he passed by Chez Madison. He'd had no right or reason to treat her so shabbily. The dark justice was she could no longer fool herself into thinking he was interested in her. No more wasted time for her. Now she could give her attention to important matters.

To her chagrin she began wondering if Rick would change his mind and assign the night charter to someone else. That possibility niggled at her mind all morning and afternoon. Later she went to Pappy's house to shower and change, and on her way back detoured three miles off Coconut Key to buy a key lime pie. She ended up buying the last two at the bakery. Halfway back to Coconut Key she glanced at the pie boxes, screamed in the privacy of her car, and pounded her fists on the steering wheel in frustration. She couldn't deny the evidence on the seat next to her; she couldn't stop thinking about him showing up at the meeting.

At eight-ten she thought she saw the *Coral Kiss* inside the horizon.

At eight-fifteen she put away the binoculars and requested his presence with a bargaining prayer. The committee, including Jiggy and the parrot, arrived instead. They all insisted on waiting for Captain Parrish.

That was twenty minutes ago. Twenty endless minutes filled with Jiggy's noisy eating, May Leigh's high-pitched laughter, Hazel Miller's endless gossip, and Rita Small's card tricks. There was nothing remotely professional about the group, unless no one had bothered to tell her they were auditioning for a television sitcom. Her thoughts kept returning to Rick.

Are you having fun out there with some pretty woman who can't bait a hook, but laughs at your jokes? And why haven't you told me any jokes?

Pressing her fingertips against her brow, Bryn scolded herself for thoughts befitting a jealous lover.

She wasn't the jealous type. And she wasn't Rick's lover. He wasn't interested anyway. She looked to a point beyond the freshly painted north rail. Beneath a big yellow moon, the inky ocean shimmered with spangles of gold light, intermittently broken by the dark clumps of tiny islands. The rustling palms framing the scene blocked her view of the channel and the twangy country and western music on the radio made it difficult to hear a boat's motor—if one happened to be trolling by.

Just how much fun are you having out there on this beautiful balmy evening, Captain? And when do I get invited out on the Coral Kiss?

Pointedly ignoring the nuzzling couple seated on the floor, she adjusted the hem of her red linen skirt and smoothed the front of its matching short-sleeved jacket. Thumbing through the ambulance brochures, she tried to interest herself in comparing the different models. This was one heck of a beginning to her first fund-raising committee meeting. From the cage on the bar, Miss Scarlett echoed Bryn's sentiments with a barrage of gravelly squawks. The unexpected noise had Bryn clutching for her heart. Enough was enough.

"I believe we've given Captain Parrish more than enough time. Let's get started," she said, reaching for the stack of folders Liza had brought by earlier.

"We ought to wait for Captain Parrish before we do anything," Hazel said, running her hand along the carved armrest of the new chair.

"Yeah. What's the rush?" Jiggy Latham asked before May Leigh scooped up the maximum amount of salsa a tortilla chip could hold and shoved the whole thing into Jiggy's mouth. Rick's lanky first mate hummed with pleasure at his current love before continuing. "We'll just have to start over when he gets here."

"If he gets here," Bryn said, then instantly regretted it. Four sets of eyes flicked their attention in her direction.

Rita Small, the owner of the Nauti-Us Swimsuit Boutique, pushed her idea list aside to flip over the playing cards in front of her. Leveling a squinty gaze across the table at Bryn, she said, "The truth, sugar pie. You and Liza weren't telling a white lie about Captain Rick being a part of this fund-raiser just to get us to join, were you?"

All four committee members leaned toward Bryn. She gave them a pulse of a smile. Friendly but professional. "Of course he's cochairing with me." Doubt prevailed in each stare directed her way. She sighed with frustration. "If you don't believe me, ask Liza." That appeared to work. They were easing back from her, mumbling contentedly.

Sorting through the folders, Bryn handed the first one to Hazel. Hazel opened it, blinked at the lists inside, then closed it. "I miss Pappy's. Don't you, Jiggy?"

Jiggy Latham's face was suddenly wistful as he stopped testing the edges of his new tattoo and looked at the wall where the mermaid mural used to be. "Yeah. We had the best times at Pappy's. Remember when the Captain bought the *Coral Kiss* and we went down to christen her?" Laughter rippled through the room, encouraging Jiggy to continue. "And the time Bill Harper dragged that fourteen-foot sailfish up the steps, plunked it on Captain Parrish's table over there, and insisted he buy it a beer?"

"Sushi grande?" May Leigh managed before collapsing in giggles across Jiggy's lap.

As laughter swelled again, Bryn couldn't deny the funky charm of Jiggy's stories. She pursed her lips to keep back a smile, then gave in to a chuckle. The rest of the group stopped laughing and looked at her. In the unnatural silence that followed, Jiggy cleared his throat.

"Can't see that happening in a place like this," he said, glancing away from the pastel plaid upholstery and over to the French impressionistic paintings leaning against the newly mirrored inner wall. "What time did Captain Parrish say he'd be here?"

"I thought you said that charter was getting back about eight or eight-thirty," Bryn said while attempting to banish the slightly guilty tone in her voice. These people could have a good time at Chez Madison too. Just a different kind of good time.

"That's right, but Captain Parrish wasn't on for that charter."

"I—I didn't know that," she said, flabbergasted by that bit of news. Where was Rick if he wasn't fishing? She made a valiant attempt to push back a tidal wave of panic. "Well, we shouldn't put off starting any longer. Wouldn't you and May Leigh like to join the rest of us up here at the table?"

"We're fine down here," he said, planting a kiss on May Leigh's head. Jiggy and Bryn each reached for the plastic pitcher of iced tea at the same time. The pitcher slipped from their struggling hands, crashing to the floor, spilling tea everywhere. In the end May Leigh's bangs were liberally splashed, and the front of Jiggy's T-shirt was lightly sprinkled, but Bryn got the worst of it. Scrambling to her feet, May Leigh took off for the ladies' room, shrieking at Jiggy in a mixture of Japanese and Spanish. Alternately swearing and apologizing in highly understandable English, Jiggy was right behind her.

Bolting out of her chair, Bryn grabbed a stack of napkins from the dessert tray and dropped to her knees to begin sopping up the spill. Although the floors had been sanded, a finishing coat of polyurethane had yet to be applied.

"For pity's sake, Jiggy, that's a fine how-do-you-do," Rita called out after him. "What'll we serve Captain Rick when he gets here?"

Bryn did her best to keep the steam from shooting out of her ears. Who cared if "Captain Rick" had anything to drink? She dropped a slice of lemon onto a soggy napkin. "Captain Rick" wasn't here. Brushing up another two slices, she set them beside the first. "Captain Rick" wasn't going to be here. Chasing ice cubes around the hardwood floor, she reminded herself that she didn't want to think where he could be.

"Bryn, sugar pie, do you have any chilly-cold beer in your Frigidaire?" Rita asked as she pushed back her chair and stood.

"Chilly-cold beer?" Bryn repeated, wondering if it was a brand name she'd never heard of. "It's possible I have some in the back."

Jiggy trailed back into the room after May Leigh. The almond-eyed woman nodded toward Bryn. "Cool. Captain Rick loves chilly-cold beer. I'll get it."

"Don't bother, May Leigh. I doubt if the Captain's going to make it here tonight. He never said for sure—"

A chorus of mutinous groans filled the room. "Well, he didn't say he wasn't coming either," she added, her hands planted flat on the floor a few inches in front of her knees.

"I said I'd come later if I could."

Four heads turned toward the familiar masculine voice. At the sound of his voice Bryn's hands stopped moving, her heart started pounding, and her body shook with every emotion she could name and a few she couldn't. Excitement over his rich baritone voice. Relief that he'd finally shown up. Thankfulness that he'd made it at all. Pure annoyance that he'd gotten himself there this late! Being held hostage to another person's schedule always irritated her, but when Rick did it, she considered it a terrorist tactic. And did he have to sneak up on her like a one-man SWAT team?

She knew the moment Rick appeared from behind the ornate screen by the stairs. The ripple of excitement in the room was almost palpable. She waited until the rest of the group finished their hero-worshipping hellos. "Good evening, Captain Parrish," she said, tossing another wet napkin onto a growing pile. Once she was sure she'd gotten control of her traitorous physical reactions, her breathy voice turned smooth. "We were just about to start . . . without you." Her hand carefully closed over the wet pile of used napkins as his polished shoes appeared in front of her. She took a cautious glance up his body. From his neatly combed sun-streaked hair, to his bronze-toned skin and sky blue eyes, he looked *GQ* perfect.

"Start what?" he asked, lowering himself to his haunches to set the empty pitcher upright. He pulled a handkerchief from inside his jacket and dabbed her chin. "A food fight?"

Chapter Eleven

FOUR

With Rick's face inches from her own, she could not miss his annoying smile. Still on her hands and knees, she allowed him a few strokes with his handkerchief before turning her chin away from his hand. He aimed for her cheek, but stopped when she sent him a warning look.

"We're not gathered here to indulge in a food fight, Captain Parrish. We're here to discuss ideas for the fund-raiser. Or did you forget?"

"No, I didn't forget," he said, handing her the handkerchief. He pointed to a drenched area between her breasts before lacing his fingers together in front of his dangling tie. "I even have an idea."

He continued smiling at her in that exasperating, in-charge, highly amused way of his. Pointedly ignoring the front of her jacket, she looked him straight in the eye while she dabbed at her cheek instead. "We can't wait to hear it."

"Yeah. What'd you have in mind, Captain Rick?" Rita asked through a hail of gum snapping. The rest of the group moved a little closer as Rick stood.

"First, let's get the cochairperson off her hands and knees." He offered Bryn his hand, and after a few hesitant seconds, she took it.

"How about a fishing tournament?"

"Of course," Millie said. "We should have known Captain Rick would come up with the right idea the first time."

"Isn't he wonderful?" Rita remarked in an adoring whisper.

Jiggy gave a singular and thoroughly energetic clap. "Amen and case closed, Captain."

"Can we go fishing now?" May Leigh asked Jiggy.

"Hold on, everyone. The case is not closed. Liza told me that Islamorada and Conch Key are both having fishing tournaments this July. We need to look for a completely different idea. Something fresh and—"

"No we don't," Rick said, cutting her off. "We have all these sport fishermen down here just waiting for a little competition. I think a tournament is the perfect answer."

"I don't," she said, pressing his handkerchief into his open hand. "The entrance fees to these tournaments are high, and I can't see how we'll make much money with at least two others going on so close to ours. Besides, we would draw even more people if we could come up with a totally new event that would pull in sponsors looking for free advertising. An event with more pizzazz than a fishing tournament," she said, looking at the others. "What do you think?"

Rita shifted her weight from one foot to the other, then looked thoughtfully at Millie while popping a large bubble.

Millie raised her eyebrows and looked at Jiggy.

Jiggy looked someplace between skeptical and confused.

And May Leigh had missed the question entirely while searching through her purse for a comb.

"More pizzazz?" Rick asked. "Don't you mean more problems for everyone here?"

"Not if we show up for meetings and work together cooperatively." The rest of the group made a series of uncomfortable sounds. A cough. A gasp. A groan. And one "Oh, my good lord!" Bryn stood her ground, then decided to advance while the others recovered from her countering response to their hero. "I believe Rita brought along a few ideas." She smiled at her. "Didn't I see a list in front of you before?"

"List? Oh, no," she said, shaking her head hard enough to fling her drop earrings into tiny orbits. "That was something else. No, I didn't have any ideas at all. Anyone else have any?"

Everyone shrugged at once, leaving Bryn to wonder if they'd rehearsed the move. Anything seemed possible when the committee turned their attention to Rick.

"I'm not ready to give up on this tournament idea, so hear me out, Bryn," Rick said. "It's still the most profitable fund-raiser I know of, and it won't run us ragged this summer. I've already spoken to the two other marinas on Coconut Key, and they both told me they'd be glad to get involved with it."

"Oh, really?" Bryn said, unbuttoning her wet jacket and pulling it off. Dropping it on the table, she whipped around to him in a fury that surprised even her. "Didn't it occur to you to speak to me before going ahead on your own?"

Shoving his blazer back, he calmly propped his hand on his hip below his belt. His friendly expression disintegrated into a series of frown lines between his brows and on either side of his blue eyes. Conviction deepened his voice. "Look, I thought this would go a lot faster for everyone if I took care of the footwork myself. I happen to know what people will go for around here. Do you have a problem with that?"

"The problem," she said, crossing her arms and stepping closer to him, "is that I've spent valuable time away from my business and the restaurant to work on several ideas. If you would have returned my calls this week, we might have figured out a way to use our time more efficiently." She ignored the whispers around her of a possible insurrection.

"We already talked about that this morning," Rick said, rubbing his thumbnail across his brow, "and I believe I told you that I've been busy."

"Well, Captain Parrish, I believe I told you the same thing."

"Ah, yes," he said, nodding as he waved his hand to indicate the rest of the room. "Painting the world yellow, I see."

She knew she could continue clashing with him over the fund-raiser indefinitely, but the moment he started in on the restaurant, something snapped inside her. Turning Pappy's Crab Shack into Chez Madison was never meant to be a situation where she had to prove her competency to anyone, especially Rick Parrish. Yet with each snafu she encountered in the restaurant project, her apprehension grew. Stooping down, she snatched the pile of wet napkins from the floor and plopped them onto the table. Ignoring the people trying to step out of the way of the splattering tea, she reached down for the pitcher and slammed it on the table. When she went after the last few pieces of unmelted ice, four sets of legs scurried for the exit.

"Sounds like you two have a bowl of wet spaghetti to straighten out, so we'll let you get to it," Rita shouted over her shoulder.

"Call us again sometime," Millie added.

Bryn was up and on her feet and hurrying after them with ice pieces cupped in her hands. "Wait! Please don't go."

"It's five-hundred-dollar night at bingo, Millie," Rita said, pulling her friend by the hand. "We can make the second half if we hurry."

"People, please! There's no need to run off. We need to talk," she shouted.

Jiggy and May Leigh didn't bother answering. They were down the steps and climbing onto Jiggy's motorcycle by the time Bryn reached the south rail.

While she continued pleading with the group, Rick started across the room. Before he was halfway there, she had dropped the ice over the railing and was slapping the wetness from her hands.

"Well, I hope you're satisfied, Captain," she said, bracing herself against the railing while she pulled off one high-heeled shoe and then the other.

"Me?" he asked, opening his hands toward her. She thrust her shoes into them and hurried around the decorative screen and down the steps. He quickly followed her. "What do you mean, you hope I'm satisfied?" He reached the bottom as Rita's rusty Mustang made the turn out of the parking lot.

"Your presence intimidated them enough to send them bolting like frightened deer." She pointed toward the taillights of Millie's late-model station wagon, which was trailing close behind Rita's car.

"Me? I wasn't the one who—" He broke off in midsentence when she stepped around him and headed back up the stairs. The best thing, he decided, was to allow her to cool off a little before having it out with her. He intended to wait a good five minutes, but instead found himself at the top of the steps staring at her before sixty seconds had elapsed.

Gliding her fingertips over a delicately carved chair, she appeared to be inspecting the new furniture for flaws. The closer he got to her, the more intense her examination became, as if she were on the verge of discovering a microscopic ding in the wood. He began wondering if the meticulous attention she was giving to the chair was a way to ignore him. Or tick him off. In an undisguised act of frustration, he dropped her shoes to the floor.

"I thought you'd have had the decency to leave by now," she said, bending closer to the top of the chair.

While he could cut off other people with a look or a gesture, these things only fueled Bryn's fire. He slammed his hand over the headrest. "Just what the hell was that all about?" he asked, moving closer.

Straightening slowly, she held her own with admirable control. "You tell me," she said in a dangerously quiet voice before cutting her eyes in his direction. "Your fan club was perfectly happy to be here until you arrived." Stepping sideways to the next chair, she began another meticulous inspection.

"I'm not talking about the committee. I'm talking about you," he said, reaching to cover one of her hands with his to keep her from moving away. His voice suddenly gentled. "And me." With her lips parting to take in more air and her breasts straining against her blouse, he noted with guilty pleasure the difficult time she was having holding herself together. Slipping her hand from under his, she reached toward the table to place an empty salsa bowl and one of the pies on a tray. Beneath her lowered lids and those incredible sable fans that passed for her lashes, her gaze moved away from him.

"What about us?" she asked in a whisper. With a deliciously slow sweep of her lashes, she cautiously looked up his arm to his mouth and then his eyes.

His heart pounded with pleasure and pain; the inevitable moment was upon him. He had to get into it and out of it without her touching any part of his soul. He smiled, knowing he could manage it. After all, he'd been *sleeping* with Sharon Burke for two years and that hadn't altered anything of importance in the secret recesses of his heart. He was simply going to kiss her. "I have this theory."

"I'm willing to listen."

Running the backs of his fingers under her chin, he lifted it as he lowered his head. From the corner of his eye he could see her curl her fingers into the key lime pie, then lift a delicious-looking gob out of the plate.

Shifting his weight, he leaned closer and suggested the wrong thing.

"You wouldn't."

As her hand arced through the air, he caught her wrist hard, sending a splatter of pie filling onto the sleeve of his blazer. Ignoring the mess, he brought her hand to his mouth and began licking her fingers. After trying to pull her hand away once, she gave up, her gaze riveted on his lips and tongue.

"We're going to have to deal with this underlying tension," he said, moving on to her palm.

Her eyelids lifted suddenly. "What are you suggesting?"

Their gazes locked as he took one of her fingers into his mouth and gave it a warm tongue bath before he answered her. "Getting a few of the kinks worked out of our systems."

"How do you intend to—" she began mumbling.

Letting go of her, he stepped back to strip off his blazer. "I think it would be better if I showed you," he said, slipping his hands around to the back of her neck and his fingers up into her hair. "Open your mouth. It'll be easier that way."

"I don't know—"

"I do."

"But—"

"Captain's orders."

Her lips parted at his whispered command.

He started the kiss with a deft stroke of his tongue along the roof of her mouth. Instantly he sensed a new tension in her. Or was it just a surprise reaction to his boldness? Either way, she was holding back. But she wouldn't be for long. He wanted one hint, one move, one shiver of invitation. Cradling the back of her head, he rotated his fingers in the soft, thick mass as he pressed himself against her breasts and belly. Like a storming pirate, he led her through the kiss, plundering her senses until he controlled them all. With each stroke of his tongue, soft nibble from his teeth, and tender brush of his lips, she responded with a broken sigh low in her throat. Victory along with a sense of relief filled his brain; this was exactly the way he wanted to experience her. Nothing complicated about it, just a bit of primal need being assuaged by a willing female.

Then something unexpected began happening. Curiosity stole quietly into the moment. A growing desire to claim more than momentary possession of her hot, sweet mouth taunted his resolve. With each of her breathy sighs he sensed a fusing of the physical and the cerebral. The effect was staggering. Dammit, he only meant to get her out of his system, but the more he kissed her, the more he wanted . . . more.

Bryn had wanted a hard, brusque, impersonal meeting of their flesh to finally put to rest the wildly erotic images filling her mind. She needed this kiss to be a resounding disappointment. She could deal with disappointment because in these matters she always had.

Disappointment was not what Rick delivered. From the moment his lips brushed hers, the kiss rode the line between deeply personal and purely seductive. With his solid being filling her arms, his maleness stirring her, and the way he moved against her, she chose the reality of the moment over the frustrating confusion of the recent past. She was tired of trying to figure out the mixed messages Rick had been sending her in the last week. Instead of stopping this, instead of pushing him away, she gave it all she had in a slow barrage of passion-evoking moves. Trying not to think about the deepening intimacy between them, she told herself their purpose was to clear the air. There would be no more kisses. Embracing the explanation, she poured her heart into the kiss, enjoying it for all it was worth. Suddenly he pulled back swearing, and by his guttural tone, she knew she was turning him on a lot faster than he wanted to be.

Lowering his forehead to hers, he got his breathing under control before he spoke. "Think we've cleared the air yet?" he asked, his hands curving confidently at her waist.

Here at last was the disappointment she'd wanted. And it had come just in time. One more stroke of his tongue, one more stroke of hers, and she would have followed him to the floor or pulled him onto the table. She was about to take the coward's way out and tell him yes, the air was now clear, when a slight trembling in his hands betrayed the discipline in his voice. The almost imperceptible vibration spoke volumes. Once again Rick Parrish thought he could keep his passionate nature hidden behind the experienced maneuvers of his mouth and tongue, and his flippant remark, but what began as an arrogant gesture had turned into a wet and hungry search for fulfillment. And it wasn't over yet.

"No, Captain Parrish, we have not cleared the air," she said, her feminine confidence brought to life in an epiphanous flash.

"You think you could do better?"

"I'll give it my best shot," she said, tracing circles on the faint shadow of his beard. She stopped. "With your permission, of course."

"I'm all yours," he said, when he was capable of speaking.

She gave him her most enigmatic smile. *Not yet, but you will be, Captain.* Sliding a fingertip over his lips, she followed the tender exploration with her tongue. His quiet struggle to remain unaffected moved her, but not enough to make her stop. Her words were a hot whisper against his lips. "I read somewhere this works a lot better if both parties are willing participants."

"Where'd you read tha—"

She cut him off with a delicate bite to his lower lip. He sucked in half a breath and held on to it like a drowning man.

"I'll lend you that book later," she said, plunging her fingers into his sun-streaked hair and giving his head a soft shake. "Right now let's get to the bottom of this 'underlying tension.' Let's get these 'kinks worked out.' "

His dead-serious expression lasted no more than a second. Maybe two. And then her world suddenly tilted on its axis. Drawing her against him, he took her mouth with heart-searing possession. Through her wanton actions she'd asked for the kiss, teased him for it, craved it, and now there was nothing to do but surrender to his wild show of passion. The determined way he was holding her, stroking her backside, molding his hands along the curves of her hips, made her want to caress the length of him. One last shred of sanity had her locking her knees to fight gravity. Or was it to fight the inexorable desire to open her body to Rick? She didn't know. She didn't care. He was tugging her blouse from the waistband and pushing up the delicate material as he lowered himself down the front of her. Just as quickly, their dance of seduction stopped when he looked up into her face. Without a word from his lips, she understood what he was asking. Poising her fingertips on his shoulders, she directed him closer with whisper-soft pressure. Rubbing his thumbs beneath her rib cage, he said her name on a sigh that sent shivers to her core. Drawing his tongue over the satin smoothness of her middle, he veered south, lavishing her navel with quick, wet licks. Tiny darts of pleasure penetrated her most sensitive places—places he wasn't touching. Yet. Moving his fingers over the moist trail he'd made with his tongue, he deepened the pleasure already there.

Alarms were going off inside her head. As sure as she was about their shared desire for each other, the idea was still brand new. She needed a little more time with it. Any second now she wouldn't have the strength to pull away. "Rick," she whispered, barely holding on to the last of her will. Slipping his hand under her skirt, he caressed the inside of her knee before moving higher up her thigh. And higher still. When he moved past the lacy top of her thigh-high stocking and brushed the silky material between her legs, she felt her knees beginning to give.

"How're we doing?" he whispered.

She tried saying his name again, but gave in to a gasp when his fingers slipped between elastic and throbbing flesh. Sinking her fingers into his hair, she held on as wave after wave of need swirled through her. If he continued his teasing strokes a bit farther and a moment longer, she would give up thinking about anything remotely rational. On the next sound, they both froze.

"*Rrrrawk!* Ohhh! Baby, baby, baby!"

Biting back a stream of curses, Rick withdrew his hand, took a steadying breath, and carefully stood up. The first thing that struck him was her wide-eyed look and the way she was wiping her mouth.

"Are you brushing off my kisses or rubbing them in?"

Blinking the dazed expression from her eyes, she began tucking her blouse back into her waistband. Another squawking salvo brought her back to her senses. "Does it matter, as long as we cleared the air?"

Dropping his head back, he laughed softly, thinking that he liked her unpredictableness, her ability to hold her own with him, and most of all, the sheer pleasure of her womanly reactions. The undeniable truth was, he liked it too damned much. Shaking his head, he was once again himself and fully aware of the reality of his life. A life where he didn't take chances with matters of the heart. "What *was* that all about?" he asked, not bothering to keep annoyance out of his voice.

"I believe we were dealing with underlying tension and working the kinks out of our systems," she said, twisting a small opal ring on her middle finger. That soft, almost lonely look began returning to her face before she had a chance to turn away. "Anyway, we gave it our best shot," she added, busily piling the rest of the refreshments onto the tray.

"Well, we blew it," he said in a storm of emotions he wanted to be rid of. Just because he was suddenly and madly consumed with having her didn't mean he couldn't control the rampant desire continuing to fire through his body. Especially if he stopped staring at her backside while she was leaning over the table.

God, how he hated this feeling of being torn between the old ways he loved and wanting Bryn. There, he'd finally been honest with himself. And it wasn't helping a thing. Rolling his eyes in frustration, he sat down in a new chair, not even bothering to look for his battered captain's chair. By now she'd probably pitched that relic along with the rest of the Crab Shack's furnishings.

For the first time since arriving, he made himself look carefully at the changes she'd made in the restaurant. That she had a flair for pulling together the perfect pieces for a first-class restaurant was obvious. The beautifully framed copies of Monets and van Goghs propped against the bar would look perfect on the banana-yellow walls of Chez Madison. But never between the beer signs at Pappy's Crab Shack.

Their eyes met in silent understanding.

"It's not like it used to be, is it?" she asked, offering a benign smile.

Shaking his head slowly, he said, "I hardly recognize the place."

Stepping away from the table, she began rubbing her palms together in that awkward yet endearing way of hers. "That's about what the others said." Rick's continued silence prickled over her skin. Clearing her throat, she walked over to the rail. Forcing a false cheerfulness into her voice, she continued. "The louvered shutters are supposed to be installed in the next few days, and the saltwater aquarium is being delivered on Tuesday." When he still didn't respond, her voice faltered, then rushed on. "I-I keep having second thoughts on the chairs. These are samples my contacts in Miami sent down for me to see. That's usually not done, but I've been doing business with them for several years. Anyway, I couldn't have chosen a more appropriate pattern. Muted plaid is much less threatening than a floral to male clientele." She knew she was talking about things that couldn't possibly interest him, but in the most maddening way she wanted his approval. And he wasn't giving it to her. "I've always believed classic styles could work well anywhere, but . . ." Trailing off, she turned to face him.

"But not for Coconut Key," he said, standing up.

Lowering her gaze to the tassels on his shoes, she tried ignoring the way he ended her sentence, then realized how foolish that would be. She couldn't erase what he'd said, especially since she'd led him into saying it. Misgivings about the future success of Chez Madison churned in her heart. Maybe she hadn't researched the demographics as thoroughly as she should have. Maybe she had ignored her usual review procedures in order to speed up the project, but there was a reasonable explanation for her actions. This was for her beloved grandfather, the man she'd missed all those years when she was growing up. She wanted the restaurant ready for Pappy Madison as quickly as possible. She glanced up at Rick as he ran his hand along the refinished bar. None of this had anything to do with him.

Stooping, he looked at the paintings and examined their frames, then walked quietly to the north rail to stare out at the old sign up by the road. More doubts nipped at her insides until she gave in to them with a painful sigh. How had this man, a stranger until a few weeks ago, affected her usual sound reasoning and her business judgment? And more importantly, how had she let this hardheaded, hard-bodied man kiss her naked navel and touch her *there* until she was shivering near the edge of a climax? She closed her eyes, remembering, stroke for stroke, every perfect sensation he'd caused within her. The memory sent thick ribbons of heat fluttering through her again, tickling her, teasing her, pulling tightly against her with unrelenting pleasure.

"Did you sell the jukebox yet?"

Her eyes flew open; he was standing inches from her. "Wh-what—oh, no. The price wasn't right."

"Phew! Glad to hear that," he said, watching her thoughtfully. "I might know of an interested party. Can I take a look at it?"

No matter what the romantics said, she didn't believe in mind reading, so Rick couldn't know what she'd just been thinking. She was safe there. Even so, she had to put distance between them or blurt out like a crazy person just how wonderful he'd made her feel.

"I had it moved to the storage room downstairs," she said, inching sideways and then heading toward the stairs.

"How much do you want for it?" he asked, following her down the stairs and into the dark storage room.

"Four thousand." Fumbling for the light switch, she sensed his solid presence moving nearer.

"Here. Let me help you," he said, brushing against her backside.

"Stay where you are. I can get it. I mean, I'm in this place all the time. I'll have it on in just a second."

He moved back. "I think it's on the other side of the door."

"Oh, right," she mumbled, stumbling over his foot.

Both of his hands closed over her arms, and he pulled her close. Faint light from the parking lot outlined his face and made his eyes shimmer. "You okay?"

"Yes," she lied, forcing a little laughter from the middle of her throat. If she didn't move away from him soon, she wouldn't bother looking for the light switch the rest of the night. "You said you might have a buyer?" she asked, moving out of his grasp to feel the wall with both hands. Harsh light suddenly flooded the room. She sent up a silent prayer of thanks before turning to look at him. "Does this buyer know how beaten up it is?"

"Yes, he does," Rick said, walking over to the machine. He ran his hands along the curved top and down over the rounded chrome. Repositioning himself, he flexed his knees before testing its weight with the flat of his hands. "I'd have to get a couple of guys to help move it." Giving it a shove, he squatted down to examine the back of it. "Mind if I plug it in?"

"Go ahead," she said, still thankful that there was space between them. What harm could playing the jukebox do to her newfound control?

After he'd made the connection, he stood up, turned his back toward her, and stretched a lazy arm across the top of the jukebox. Colored light bubbled through the clear tubing decorating the front. After a moment he pulled a coin from his pocket, dropped it into the slot, and made his selection.

For reasons she couldn't begin to fathom, his familiarity with and total attention to the jukebox irritated her. If she had to put a name to it, she felt jealous. Knowing that irritated her more than ever. The next thought popped into her head like an exploding cherry bomb, small but drawing enough attention to warrant a fast response. "You're the buyer. Why? I mean, what could you possibly want with that old jukebox?"

He looked her up and down in that way that said "Watch out, you're getting close to a nerve." The jukebox clattered and clicked. Without warning, his expression warmed to a forgiving smile as he turned fully around to her. Shaking his head in a show of sweet appreciation, he reached behind him to pat the machine. "Helluva lot of good memories attached to this."

"Really?" She could feel warning flares igniting inside her.

"You'd have to have knocked back a few beers with it playing in the background to know."

"I see. Is that another way of telling me I don't understand how Coconut Key works?" Listening to herself, she was starting to feel as if she had several personalities inhabiting her. None of them sounded very nice, and all of them were eager to show themselves this evening.

"I didn't say that, Bryn," he said, his voice irritatingly even.

"Everyone's so ready to tell me how great the past was that no one wants to talk about the future. What's wrong with you people? Don't you know the future's just a place, a time to make more memories?"

"Is that what you want, Bryn? To make a few memories?"

The first notes of a Michael Bolton song spilled into the fragile silence between them. Staring over his shoulder, she concentrated on a painting of dogs playing billiards, and when he pushed off the jukebox, she shifted her stare to a stack of soft-drink boxes. As he crossed the room, sparklers replaced the cherry bomb and the flares, filling her with prickles of anticipation. He eased her gently into his arms.

"Let's do it, Bryn."

"Do what?" she whispered.

Swaying her, he moved her smoothly into a dance step. With his hand firmly on the small of her back, he gave her a tender smile. "Let's make a memory."

Yes, let's make a memory, she thought as she laid her cheek on his shoulder. A rich and real memory, not a fantasy substitute. She already had too many of those with him. She moved with him then, as if they'd danced this way every Saturday night at some out-of-the-way roadhouse. The song went on, intimate and suggestive and unlike the kiss they'd shared earlier, making her acutely aware that, unlike the jukebox, she had no history with him. And no understanding of what should happen next. All they shared was a deep disagreement about the future and enough sexual energy for spontaneous combustion to occur. Any second now.

Rick moved closer on the same note she did, his exhalation turning into a sigh along with hers. From where he was dancing, he could see out the door and across the parking lot. Bled of life and half hidden in the palms up by Marina Road, Pappy's old neon sign was barely readable. Soon that would be removed, becoming another faint memory of what his life once was. He looked down at Bryn, stirring the hair on her forehead with his breath. Was she to blame for reopening the old wounds? Could this armful of sweet woman be his worst enemy? What did he know about her? That she was changing his world in ways that broke his heart. That she could bristle the hair on the back of his neck with one look. That he couldn't think straight from wanting to know her like no other man could. The song ended, but he couldn't give her up that fast. He continued holding her while the stillness and quiet brought them back into reality.

Pulling away from him, she tucked her hair behind her ears, then adjusted the buttons on her blouse. With her gaze darting nervously around the room, she said, "We ought to be discussing this fund-raiser, you know."

Flustered and mussed and enchanting, she went on and on about their responsibilities. He ached for her more than he thought humanly possible, but what he saw when her darting amber eyes settled on his was enough to rock his soul. The biggest and neediest charity wasn't the ambulance fund, it was the emptiness of their own lives.

FIVE

In the surreal shimmer of the jukebox's bubbling lights, Rick had a sudden impulse to lean in close to Bryn and whisper, *"Shhh. It's late and we could be putting this time to better use. What do you say we go back to my place and talk about our kinks. Then we can deal with this underlying tension until the sun comes up. Hell, Bryn, let's find a few new kinks and work on them too."*

Torrid scenes, taking place below a mirrored ceiling and over every square inch of red satin sheets, captured his mind. He pictured his meticulous exploration of her nakedness as she writhed in sensual abandon beneath his attentive mouth. The feel of her giving, wanting body spurred him on to discover that secret place that quivered at the touch of his tongue. When she couldn't bear another moment, when she cried out for him, he planted himself inside her and ended their emptiness in quick, hot strokes. All she had to do was give him the go-ahead and he'd redefine sexual fulfillment for the both of them. This need to have her was, after all, about a shared desire for erotic release, those strange moments of tenderness notwithstanding. If he began to doubt that, he had only to remember the needy way she responded to his tongue against her belly and his fingers against her slick heat. But he wasn't going to push it tonight. Too much had happened, and when their time together came, he wanted her total focus.

Lifting his fingers to her lips, he silenced her complaints about a fishing tournament with a soft "Shhh. It's late and we could both use some time out. What do you say we get together tomorrow after my last charter? We can talk about your new idea for the fund-raiser over dinner." Removing his hand from the velvet warmth of her lips, he moved to unplug the jukebox. He said teasingly, "That is, if you can come up with a good idea by then."

When he turned around to her again, she was taking her hand away from her lips. The sensual gesture replicated his own a moment before. The idea of her need to touch herself where he had touched her made his straining erection ache.

"Not tomorrow, Rick," she said, hastily moving toward the wall to turn off the overhead light. "I have to go up to Miami to see a client. And I'll be busy for the next few days because—"

"Just tell me when we can get together," he said in a way that refused to hear another excuse. Playing tickle and run couldn't go on forever. If she wanted games, he would oblige, but only when they were both buck naked.

"I'm trying to figure out when we can, but I really do have a scheduling problem. I hate asking anyone for help, but I need a strong man for this. Maybe two strong men."

There she goes, he thought, as he followed her out the door, *stirring the flames inside me with those sable lashes, soft voice, and never-ending images*. "Name it." *But forget about two strong men. What needy, greedy thing can I do for you?*

"Rick, they're about to start physical therapy with my grandfather, but first they're going to let him come home for a short visit. He's been threatening to sneak out and wheel himself back up the Overseas Highway if they don't oblige him. Would you help me with him tomorrow?"

He nodded, snorting uncomfortably at himself. What the hell had gotten into him? Was he so in lust for her that he would interpret everything and anything she said as a lead-in to sex? Had it been that long since he'd lost himself inside a woman's tight softness?

"Of course I'll help you with him," he said, closing the door to the storage room.

"That's great. You see, I can't bring him upstairs in a wheelchair by myself, and I know he'll want to see what I've done up here," she said, starting up the stairs.

"Bryn?"

"Yes?" she said, turning around to him.

Planting a foot on the second step, he curved his hand around his knee and angled himself toward her. "Have you considered the possibility that he won't be pleased with what you've done up there?" Her smile deflated to a blank stare. He could feel her withdrawing in that way a woman did when a man least wanted or needed her to.

Staring at the steps separating them, she appeared to wait until the question melted away in the strained silence. "Do you want the jukebox, Rick?"

"The jukebox?" Standing straight, he lowered his foot to the landing. Nodding, he slipped his hands into his trouser pockets. "Yes. Yes, I do. I'll drop the check in your mailbox and have the thing out of your way by the time you get back from Miami. Pappy gave me an extra set of keys to this place. Is that okay with you?"

"That'll be fine," she said, before running her tongue over the edges of her teeth. He thought she was about to say something or ask him something, but with an almost imperceptible shake of her head, she said, "Good night, Rick," then fled upstairs.

Next afternoon, despite the perfect weather, his easygoing customers, and the knowledge that Pappy Madison would be coming home for a visit, Rick was feeling decidedly uneasy as he headed over to Pappy's. All the quirky pieces of his recent history kept bumping together like unrelated flotsam. He prided himself on a clear head, so his scattered thoughts irritated him. By five that afternoon, after slamming mackerel, yellowtail snapper, and grouper onto the display spikes, then posing beneath the day's catch with his smiling customers for the obligatory snapshots, he'd finally figured it out. The weighty combination of his recent visit to Angie's parents, accepting that the Crab Shack was gone, finding out about Pappy's injury, and ending his relationship with Sharon, had shaken his once uncomplicated world.

Then there was Bryn.

Despite their strong differences of opinion, he knew the sexual attraction between Bryn and him could not be denied. He knew it as well as he knew his reef charts. As for the rest of Bryn's life, that was none of his business. Especially the mess over the restaurant conversion. If she insisted on demolishing Pappy's Crab Shack simply to hang a few copies of Monet and serve expensive wine, so be it. When she left Coconut Key, and she would, he would see what he could do to help Pappy.

In the meantime, if she wanted to wrap those gorgeous legs around him and sail off with him to heaven for a few lost hours, he could accept that too. But that was it! All he wanted was to feel the pressure of her knees hugging his hips, to see her head thrown back in ecstasy, and to hear her crying out with pleasure before he melted into her essence.

"Cripes, Pappy, what have they been feeding you in that hospital? Stones?" Rick asked while he and Jiggy carried the old man in his wheelchair up the stairs.

"Tasted like stones. Careful you don't flip me out of this," he said, his knuckles tense and white on the armrests.

From the restaurant's upper entrance, Bryn bit back advice, but gave in to the urge to direct the maneuvers with her hands. When they lowered the wheels to the floor and set the brake, she breathed a loud sigh of relief.

"*Rrrrawkk!* Oh, baby, baby, baby!"

Pappy turned to his right to look at Jiggy. "You had Miss Scarlett at your place, didn't you?"

"Hey, Pappy. How'd you know that?" Jiggy asked, nervously patting the old man's arm.

"Because the evangelist I got her from never taught Miss Scarlett anything but scripture. And I wouldn't let anyone talk that way around her." Pappy slapped Jiggy's hand away. "I leave for a while, and when I get back, my bird's talking like she's been watching the Playboy channel. Is there nothing sacred anymore? And look at Bryn. She's red as Miss Scarlett's feathers!"

Just when Bryn thought she'd survive the flashback to Rick's total body kiss, Miss Scarlett let loose with another bawdy line. Bryn stole a quick glance in Rick's direction, and even though he was laughing with the others, his knowing gaze was there to meet hers. He had to be remembering that hot moment when his fingers came close to entering her. As insane as it seemed, his laughing with the others was the only acceptable thing he could do. The only acceptable thing *she* could do was roll her eyes in mock disapproval and wait for someone to change the subject. That someone was Rick.

"Come on, Jiggy, we've got work to do. Pappy, give me a call when you want to come down. We'll be over in a minute."

Bryn didn't know whether to feel relieved or hurt when Rick didn't look at her again before he headed down the stairs behind his employee. There were other, more important matters to concern herself with, she chided herself. "Ready, Grandfather?" she asked, getting behind his wheelchair.

"Am I ever!" he said, clapping his hands together.

Her hands were shaking as she rolled him around the screen carved with egrets and ibises and into the dining room. What she had to show him wasn't the macaroni necklace she'd made for him at age five or the pie-tin crown she'd presented him that last Christmas before he left, but all things being equal, she felt the same anxiety. Heck, exacting real estate moguls in New York didn't produce this much trepidation. "Now, Grandfather, it's not finished. Those chairs are getting returned to the store because there's too much yellow in the room. Yellow is a very uplifting, cheerful color, but too much is too much." Pappy Madison wasn't saying a thing. "Try picturing tables filled with people, and piano music playing softly in the background." She kept on talking, knowing she was filling her need to justify the changes more than his need to understand the particulars. Pangs of desperation filled her chest, and no matter how cleverly she tried steering his thoughts, the moment of truth couldn't be put off any longer. Coming around the side of the chair, she squatted down by his good leg and patted it with a shaky hand. "Go on, you can tell me what you think. Be honest, Grandfather."

The old man leaned forward in his chair, steepling his fingers and pressing them against his mouth. Bryn attempted to read his reaction by studying the steady blue gaze beneath furry white brows. When her fears kept creeping in, she gave up, shut up, and waited. After a while he leaned back and grinned.

"Girl, you've been working awfully hard, haven't you?"

She nodded, trying to weigh the ambiguous remark in her favor with a matching grin. Both of their smiles, she realized, were strained attempts to please each other. She felt a sinking sensation in her stomach.

"Yes, and I've enjoyed doing it for you, Grandfather."

"Hmm. Rick still giving you a ration about it?"

Standing slowly, she walked the few feet to the carved screen and began tracing the pencil-thin legs of an ibis with her fingertip. "He believes Chez Madison is too upscale for Coconut Key," she said, turning back to her grandfather. "You'd think he had a financial interest in the place."

Pappy Madison tugged on the wheels on his chair, turning himself first to the left and then the right. He cleared his throat noisily.

"He'd never admit it, Brynnie, but in a way he does have a financial interest."

"What?" She walked quickly back to the chair. "What are you saying? Is Rick your silent partner? Is that why he's so . . ." She stopped to think of the right word " . . . opinionated?" A huge range of new problems suddenly loomed as she considered his involvement. She settled down on her heels beside the old man again. "Is it?"

"Nothing formal as that. In fact, he'd be the first to insist he had nothing to do with Pappy's Crab Shack, but if it weren't for Rick, this place most likely would be just another expensive souvenir shop in a resort complex."

"But why?" she asked, dipping into that guarded well of curiosity, the one marked Rick.

"Remember a few years back when you didn't make it down for a visit because you took that business trip to Hong Kong? Well, Hurricane Lula paid us a visit instead. She didn't do diddly-squat to the rest of Florida, but she practically destroyed the Middle Keys. Until that happened, I'd been living in a fool's paradise and hadn't increased my insurance as I should have. A lot of us hadn't. I was about to give up and go live in the back country. Rick showed up with his checkbook and helped me put this place back together. He helped out just about everyone along Petticoat Channel. Of course, we've paid him back since then."

"Other people? He's never mentioned any of this to me," she said.

"Are you surprised at that, Brynnie?"

"I don't know enough about him, at least about his past, to be surprised one way or the other. Most of our conversations consist of shouting matches over the fund-raiser, or this place." She swallowed and looked away, remembering their other modes of communication. *Sometimes we don't talk at all.* Before the hot images could take over, she rushed on to another subject. "Does he make that much money off the fishing charters and boat slip rentals, or is he independently wealthy?"

Pappy eyed her carefully. "You told me you didn't want to hear about Rick. Have you changed your mind?"

Slowly getting to her feet, she pulled up a chair and sat down in front of her grandfather. "No, I haven't changed my mind. Just tell me about him where it concerns you and the restaurant," she said.

"Representatives from a major hotel chain came in the day after the storm and offered everyone on this side of Coconut Key big bucks for their properties, or what was left of their properties. Let me tell you, Brynnie, people were torn in several different directions. Some wanted off the island for good, so those big offers looked mighty tempting; others simply didn't have the insurance to start rebuilding. I'm not talking about big businesses. I'm talking about the bathing suit shop, that mom-and-pop motel, you know, places like that. Ah, Brynnie, it was a terrible mess all around." The old man reached toward his elevated leg, rubbing the top of his thigh in silence.

"How are you feeling? Is your leg bothering you?"

Pappy continued staring at the place where the jukebox had been. "I'm okay." After a while, he looked up at Bryn as he slid a knuckle under one eye. "If we hadn't had Rick Parrish call that meeting at his house and insist everyone hold off making a decision for a few weeks, I don't know where we'd be today. He reminded us that we had a special piece of the American dream down here and that once we gave it up, we'd never get it back. He said those of us lucky enough to have children and grandchildren wouldn't be able to look them in the eye when they found out we sold out to a corporation. Reps from the hotel chain showed up at Rick's during another one of his meetings and tried taking it over. They yapped on and on that prosperity was sure to come for all of us in the wake of their bulldozers. When they handed Rick a check for his marina property, the whole room went dead silent. Guess those reps thought if they could get Rick, they'd have all of us." The old man paused to remember. Shaking his head, he said in a fierce whisper, "Damn, what a man."

What a man indeed, she thought, finally understanding why Rita and Millie and virtually everyone else she'd met had nothing but praise and adoration for Rick Parrish. He'd kept his head when the rest of them were consumed with fear. He'd stood up to big business and conquered them at their own game. He'd even taken money from his own pocket to back his cause. What she didn't understand was the reason behind Rick's legendary stand against the interlopers. It would be easy enough to ask her grandfather, but somehow she knew the answer had to come from Rick himself. "What happened next?"

Her grandfather winked. "You don't think he backed down, do you? No siree. He tore up the check, tossed it over his deck rail, and showed them the quickest way off the key." Waving toward the breezy palms and the sparkling ocean, he said, "You see, Rick knew we'd all regret it if we sold out this place. Thank God he wasn't in shock like the rest of us. He knew when to rally us, and even when a few looked as if they were going to cave, he was there with an understanding ear. Hell, Brynnie, he even put his money where his mouth was."

"How did he come up with enough?"

"I don't know and it didn't seem right to ask. And now it's not important because it's all paid back." He caught her gaze and held it steady. "At least, it's not important to me, Brynnie."

His cryptic silence had her more curious than ever, but the old man's shoulders were rounded with fatigue. And if she wanted to know more, she could ask Rick. Leaning forward in her chair, she took his hands in hers. "You're tired, aren't you?"

"A tad."

"I'll call Rick and Jiggy to come help us get you down the steps and back to your own bed. We never should have come straight here from the hospital." She was halfway to the phone behind the bar when he called to her.

"Brynnie, wait up."

"Yes?" she said, turning toward the odd tone.

"Why don't you walk over. I'd like to be alone here for a while, if you don't mind."

"Okay," she said, staring at his profile as he wheeled himself across the room. He'd never looked older or smaller or lonelier than he did at this moment. Tears stung the backs of her eyes. She moved past him toward the stairs, but couldn't resist squeezing his shoulder. He caught her hand and pressed it to his cheek. "Brynnie, where's the jukebox?"

"I sold it."

His chin came up and he looked away. "Oh," he managed to whisper before swiping his nose with his other hand. "I'm sure it's still making music somewhere."

"Rick bought it."

The old man's head swiveled in her direction. "He did?" His shocked expression disappeared into a grin before laughter cackled out of him. "I should have known," he said, slapping his good leg. "That's good."

Why that pleased her grandfather so much, she didn't know. The important thing was hearing him laugh for the first time since she'd wheeled him into the dining room. Otherwise she wouldn't have been able to leave him, and hide her own tears as she made her way down the stairs and through the palm grove toward Rick's marina.

SIX

Two days later Rick couldn't get his mind off Bryn. She'd been strangely quiet the few times he'd managed to be in her presence, leaving him to worry if she was avoiding him for a particular reason. Realizing how consumed he was by her, he did what he always did when he felt the world coming a little too close. He dragged his telescope onto his back deck, angled it high over the water, and tried losing himself in another part of the Milky Way.

Tonight after sunset every commonplace sound broke into his escape plan. Screaming gulls, the dinging bell on his microwave, and the far-off buzz of an outboard motor caused him to lose his concentration and his steady hand. These were all momentary and forgettable distractions, he told himself. *Just like she was.* He began breathing easier as they melted into the background. Just as he reached the edge of the galaxy, he heard the sound of an approaching car. Moving back from the telescope's eyepiece, he felt a warning prickle across his shoulders. No one drove to the end of Marina Road unless they wanted to see him. Skidding back his chair, he walked to the edge of his upper deck, prepared to deal quickly with the uninvited visitor. Until he saw who it was.

Bryn appeared in the side yard carrying a dry-cleaning bag over her shoulder. She stopped next to a weed-filled planter before looking up at him with a tentative smile.

"You forgot your blazer again."

Worse than that, I forgot to make love to you, he thought. Shifting uncomfortably under his stare, Bryn gave in to an embarrassed wince. Removing her sunglasses from the top of her head, she said, "You have company, don't you? I'm sorry, I should have called first." When she started back to the driveway, he quickly motioned for her to join him.

"Don't go. I'm alone," he said.

Her shoulders instantly relaxed while genuine relief smoothed her brow. Cripes, what did she think was going on at the end of Marina Road? Drug smuggling? Seances? Nightly orgies? "What's up?" he asked. "Did my check for the jukebox bounce?"

Lifting the plastic-covered dry-cleaning over her shoulder, she walked toward the stairs laughing. Thank God for that tall flight of stairs. Otherwise he wouldn't have time to take in her splendid details. Her hair, which once reminded him of fiery sunbursts, tumbled and bounced in soft curves around her head. Beneath her cherry-colored T-shirt, her full breasts jiggled just enough to cause his lips to part in breath-stealing appreciation. As she moved closer he grimaced with masculine approval. Not simply a T-shirt, a *cropped* T-shirt. She was definitely out to get him tonight.

Rick felt the smile, or at least the beginning of one, lifting one corner of his mouth. She'd come to Coconut Key unannounced. She'd shown up in his dreams with amazing regularity. Why should he be surprised that she was moving up his stairs like a blithe spirit? Or an angel taking flight with that plastic bag flapping behind her. A very determined angel out to capture his soul, if he let her.

"I cashed your check a few days ago," she said. "No problem."

There was too a problem. A terribly wonderful problem that made his heart thump twice as fast when he imagined trying to solve it. Her pebbly nipples were poking against her shirt, presenting him with a troublesome question. Was she or wasn't she wearing a bra? The only way he could know for certain was by a firsthand examination.

He forced himself to raise his gaze, but he didn't get very far. The embroidered blossoms skimming across her perfect cleavage were an irresistible invitation to keep on staring at her breasts. He hadn't pulled petals off a flower in years, but he was willing to give it a try tonight. "Nice flowers," he murmured as she arrived near the top of the steps.

"Thanks. I bought this outfit this morning at Rita's shop," she said, reaching to hang the bag on a hook above one of the three sets of French doors.

Up went the hem of her T-shirt, exposing the velvety smooth, tautly muscled place above her waistband. The place he'd tracked with his tongue. He could drop to his knees and do it all again, but this time that love-hungry moment wouldn't be the final act of a kiss gone crazy. If he had his way, it would be a prelude to the wildest night of their lives. All she had to do was ask.

"Rick, I need to ask you for a favor."

His gaze flicked to her face. He didn't believe she could read his mind, but recognizing the pressing evidence behind his fly was another matter. With an inward sigh he sent up a prayer of thanks. She was looking over his shoulder, and she was as tense as he'd ever seen her. Without warning, his roguish ideas disappeared, replaced with a rush of compassion. Her tentative, nervous expression was altogether out of character for the Bryn Madison he'd come to know.

"Is everything all right?"

She ran her hand along the thick pipe railing, patting a bubble of gleaming white paint. There was something about her hands and fingers that usually inspired erotic images for him, but her uneasiness overshadowed those pictures tonight. Working her fingers without a plan, she stroked the pipe, then lightly drummed her palms against it.

"Is it Pappy, Bryn? Is there something—"

"No, no. Grandfather's fine. They'll be starting his physical therapy tomorrow."

"That's good to hear," he said, pulling up a teakwood deck chair for her. "The visit home must have been good for him."

Moving her head and shoulders in an unconvincing shrug, she turned toward the water, grasping the pipe rail with both hands this time. "That's part of the reason I came by tonight," she said looking out toward the mangroves covering half the shore.

Sensing her deepening tension, he waited quietly, concentrating on the way she raised her eyes toward the pastel light on the horizon. As she grappled with her troubles, the tension showed in her profile. A warning prickle zipped between his shoulder blades for the second time in five minutes. He crossed his arms, fighting the desire to pull her near and kiss the strained expression from her mouth. He looked over the rail at the snarl of mangrove roots. He was not going to get involved with the personal details of Bryn's life. He'd stayed clear of those things with Sharon Burke, and that relationship had served its purpose. Of course, Sharon had never wanted to talk about personal things. He stared harder at the mangrove roots, fighting the next thought. Rolling his eyes, he gave in with a sigh. Okay, so Bryn wasn't Sharon Burke. Maybe he'd give on that rule just this once. "Talk to me, Bryn," he said quietly. "Tell me what's bothering you."

Making a fist, she thumped on the rail before turning back to him. "I want you to know that coming to you like this wasn't easy for me. But after talking with Grandfather and thinking hard and long about things, I decided there was no one else I could turn to." Pressing her fingers over the soft fullness of her breasts, she said, "Rick, it had to be you."

Lighthearted music from the old song played through his mind while visions of her smiling face hovered near his. He shoved his hand halfway through his hair, stopping when she whispered his name.

"Rick . . . ?"

Was he turning into a romantic fool? What was going on with her, and why was he suddenly caring about it so much? Hell, she'd probably figured out a theme for the ambulance fund-raiser and wanted to run it by him. No, she was too upset for that. Maybe it had to do with Pappy's stay in the hospital. "Bryn, does Pappy need money? Do you?"

"Oh, Rick, no. Nothing like that." She reached to press her fingers against his arm, warming him all over with a light stroke of her fingertips. When she touched him like that, it was all he could do not to fold his arms around her.

"Grandfather told me about how you helped him out after the hurricane." Her hand slipped away, and he was suddenly missing her even though she was inches from him.

"It's not money this time," she said, sinking down onto the end of the deck chair. Her hesitation returned; she rubbed her chin. When she finally raised her head to look at him through those impossibly thick lashes, he could feel her sizing him up. Whatever it was that she was going to ask him had her fidgeting with her glasses, circling her knees with them, and then twirling them until she accidentally let go. They landed with a clatter at his feet.

"Better spill it," he said, reaching to pick them up in the same moment she did. Her T-shirt slipped off one shoulder, and he forgot how to breathe. Their hands met, but he wouldn't let go of the glasses. Neither would she. He was close enough to her to nibble a wet string of kisses from the top of her arm to that tender spot below her ear. Close enough to kiss those few golden freckles scattered there like the fragile light of a comet's tail. Close enough to think she wanted him to do those things, and more. He sucked in a breath. Maybe she didn't want those things from him. Maybe he was reading too much into his own desire for her. In the strange light she appeared half fantasy, half reality, and all wanting, giving woman. If he didn't get hold of himself, he'd make the first move. But the first move had to be hers, because he had to be certain she wanted him as much as he wanted her.

With a nonchalance he didn't feel, he slid the T-shirt back onto her shoulder. What he wanted to do was pull off the cherry-colored material and cover her breasts and belly with hungry, hot kisses. His throat ached at the next thought, a thought he'd been fighting since the moment he saw her in his side yard. He hadn't been with a woman on this deck since Angie died. Suddenly he let go of the sunglasses, and she moved back to the edge of the deck chair.

"What do you want, Bryn?"

"I need your help."

"My help? With what?"

After two false starts and a series of darting glances, she looked up at him. "I need your help with the restaurant."

He cocked his head as if he hadn't heard her quite right. "You're joking, right?" he asked, before giving in to silent, shoulder-shaking laughter. So it was that damn restaurant again.

"Yeah," she mumbled, clicking the earpieces together. Her nervous gesturing wound down until she carefully folded the glasses and set them underneath the deck chair. "I mean, no." Pushing up from the chair, she moved away from him. "You were right. I was wrong, Rick. I never should have attempted such a drastic makeover of the Crab Shack." Walking alongside the rail, she stopped when she reached the spot where the telescope jutted over it. "Go ahead and laugh. I know you think I deserve it, and maybe I do," she said quietly.

"Sorry, but this is the last thing I ever thought I'd hear from you." More importantly, in the matter of self-preservation, it was the last thing he *wanted* to hear. He'd been longing for a steamy session of hot sex, but he could no longer deny she rattled him higher up, where it counted more. Proud and accomplished as she was, and as much as it cost her to come to him, she was willing to put all that aside to do the right thing. Her generous spirit was larger and more powerful than any of his own selfish goals. He wanted her in his bed, but he wanted her there on his terms. And he wanted the Crab Shack the way it was. He struggled to keep his focus on his goals. It was the only way he could survive, the only way he could keep his life of the last five years alive.

"What do you think I could help you with? Picking out finger bowls? Checking to see that your customers are wearing their ties?" he asked, keeping an edge to his voice in case he'd read her wrong. *Argue with me, dammit!*

She struck him again with a pulse of a smile.

"No," she said, avoiding his eyes as she ran both hands over the telescope's sleek barrel. "There aren't going to be any tie-wearing customers expecting sliced lemons in their finger bowls."

A new kind of tension gripped him. Was she leaving Coconut Key? He had no defenses for this kind of assault. She was bringing him to his knees with her humility. "You're giving up, Bryn?"

"Rick, I watched my grandfather's reaction when I wheeled him into the dining room. Chez Madison is not what he wants. He never told me that, but I know." Bowing her head, she twisted a small ring around her middle finger as her voice trailed off. "And I think I've known that for a long time."

Bryn sensed the moment he dropped his first shield. With everything to gain and nothing to lose, she closed the space between them. She reached out to his hand resting on the deck rail, covering it with her own.

"Help me, Rick. I want all of his friends to feel welcome there, but no more beer-soaked tables, no more peanut shells ankle deep on the floor. I want to make the Crab Shack better. Help me find a middle ground."

"Why me?"

"Because you care. No, don't roll your eyes when I say that. You spent a considerable amount of your own money rebuilding other people's businesses after the hurricane."

"I did that to protect Coconut Key from turning into just another slick resort."

"Not only for that, Rick."

"What? I did it to help out a few friends."

"And?"

"I give up. Is there something else I'm not telling you?"

"Yes," she said, nodding.

"Really?"

"Rick, you wanted your bar back then too."

"All right," he conceded. "I wanted the bar back then. Hell, I want it back now."

"So does my grandfather. So does everyone." When he didn't speak, she let go of his hand. "You know, I actually thought I was changing Pappy's Crab Shack for my grandfather's benefit. Somewhere, my stubborn pride got in the way of common sense and sound reasoning. And I hate to admit this, but I wanted to prove something to you too."

He jerked his head in her direction.

"Anyway," she continued, "I know I have to make things right again, but I'll be darned if things are going back exactly the way they were." His smile sent her confidence soaring. "When I think about Pappy's Crab Shack and the way it was, I know I can still—"

"Change it."

"Improve it, Rick."

"Change it," he said.

"I think we're into semantics here. Everything changes sooner or later, but my radical approach was wrong. What I need to understand are the subtleties of Pappy's Crab Shack."

"Subtleties? There's never been anything subtle about that place, Bryn."

"You know what I mean. Those quirks that made it cozy. The funky flavor that made you laugh." When he didn't say anything, she decided to back off and give him a moment to get used to her idea. "Anyway, will you think about it? About helping me make Pappy's Crab Shack better than before?"

Rick rested both arms against the rail as she returned to the telescope and took his place on the stool. He watched her take her sighting through the eyepiece.

She could have gone on with her plans for the restaurant, and sooner or later she would have turned a profit. But rather than hold fast to the wrong idea and take the chance of breaking Pappy's heart, she'd decided to drop the selfish reasons and do the right thing.

A comforting warmth spread through his chest as he felt himself needing to be closer to her. Joining her at the telescope, he basked in the new sensations she had inspired. He watched her from the corner of his eye with admiration and curiosity. "Making wishes?" he asked after a while.

"Yes," she said, adding her whispery voice to the rustling palms and sea sounds surrounding them. "Of course, I'm probably making them on planets instead of stars. I can never tell the difference." Laughing at herself, she lifted her face from the telescope, one eye still closed. "Do you think they'll come true anyway?" Waiting for his answer, she opened her eye.

New stars were forming in the dusky blue heaven behind her. Dozens of them. All shimmering and new and somehow brave in the darkened sky. Tonight they almost seemed close enough to touch. He slipped his fingers into the curls beside her face. "They have to be stars."

"Well, let's see if they were," she said, gliding her hand along his arm, then pressing it over his. "I wished for your help with the restaurant."

He nodded, moving his thigh between hers in a quiet act of masculine assertion. "You got it. What else?"

"I wished that you would kiss me." Running her teeth along her bottom lip, she left inviting wetness there. "How'd I do on that one?"

Blown away by her frank invitation, he filled his arms with her. "Good call." Starting with a gentle brush of her lips, he delved past them, exploring her interior with a lazy tongue. She welcomed his invasion with tender nibbles that elicited a deep and immediate groan from him. When he moved his thigh against her, he made his own wish that she understood he wasn't playing any longer. Her quick intake of air told him she got the message. Sliding his hands beneath the hem of her T-shirt, he moved his fingertips over the satin-smooth skin around her navel, then skimmed them around to the small of her back. With a slight pull he invited her to come closer. He felt the squeeze of her thighs on his before she settled her feminine center high on his leg and began rocking herself against the taut muscles. When he felt the damp heat of her erotic embrace, he pressed his thigh upwards and swore for control.

"One more wish, Rick . . ." Her whispered words unraveled to a desperate plea. "Just one more."

She didn't have to tell him. He knew. He'd always known. "Bryn, you chose all stars tonight," he said, withdrawing his leg and lifting her into his arms, "because the last wish is about to come true."

He carried her through a set of French doors and into his bedroom, stopping twice to kiss her. With her lavishing his neck and chest with nipping kisses, he somehow made it to the bed. Lowering her to her feet, he reached around her hip. "Don't worry, I have protection. It's right here," he said, tearing open the nightstand drawer and shuffling through the contents. "Somewhere."

His hasty search stopped like a freeze frame when he felt her fingers working the snap on his shorts. If she touched his hot, hard flesh, if she stroked him once, he'd spill himself.

"Rick?"

The answer came before he did. "The bathroom," he said, reluctantly setting her away from him. Of course the pack of condoms was in the bathroom. He kept condoms there because he hadn't used them in this bedroom in years. The short time it took to find the pack and return to the bedroom gave him back a modicum of control. A modicum of control quickly relinquished when he saw what was waiting for him.

Holding a corner of the sheet between her legs, Bryn was kneeling naked in the center of his bed, looking straight at him when he walked back through the door. Words caught in his throat, words he soon forgot. All he could think about were the mixed messages he was receiving. Even though she'd just stripped off her clothes in record time, she was covering herself with that white sheet like a timid virgin on her wedding night.

Dragging the sheet to her breastbone, she clutched both handfuls to her body. One tightened nipple peeked from behind rumpled white cloth. "Say something, or I'll die of embarrassment."

"Okay," he said, tossing the condoms on his nightstand. Propping his hands on his hips, he smiled. "Drop the sheet."

She blinked those thick lashes at him, then opened her eyes as wide as possible. "Now? Just like that?"

"We don't want rose petals and raindrops," he said, shaking his head. Walking closer to the bed, he continued talking softly. "Not tonight, Bryn. Tonight we want thunder and lightning. Am I right?"

Bryn licked at her lips, striving to understand this new excitement racing through her. He gave her a long, hot look that scorched her with its blazing honesty. "Rick, I've tried," she said, her voice earnest with desperation and apology. "But I've never had the thunder and lightning, and . . ."

"Go on."

"I want it, Rick. So badly . . . I want it with you," she said, watching him remove his shirt and toss it over his shoulder.

"Bryn, drop the sheet," he said, sitting down on the edge of the wide bed.

Her grasp continued tightening on the sheet until he started that daring smile. Tanned skin crinkled at the corners of his eyes, drawing attention to the wicked yet humorous light there. Delicious promises radiated from every pore of his magnificent body. The moment suddenly hummed with rightness.

She didn't drop the sheet. She lowered it slowly, her confidence building with each revealed inch. By the time she bunched it over the apex of her thighs, she'd accepted his challenge without understanding the full measure of it.

"What else do you want?" he asked, reaching for her beaded nipple, but drawing his fingers down between her breasts instead.

"I want the rose petals and raindrops too."

When she began trailing her fingers after his, he swallowed hard. "Do it again," he whispered.

"Like this?" she asked, skimming a thumb over her nipple before repeating the stroke along her body.

By following his lead, she'd discovered the way to tap into his passion. Soon he wouldn't be able to hold back what he'd so carefully guarded. The knowledge excited her, making her want to please him in ways she'd only imagined. Pushing the sheet away, she leaned back on a bank of pillows. "This too?" she asked, touching her thighs this time.

He swore under his breath, threatening the heavens if she didn't stop it, then threatening the heavens if she did. She didn't stop. She kept on stroking, taking her cues from his darkening eyes and his deepening breaths. When he stood and removed the rest of his clothing, she invited him closer with the whisper of his name.

"Rick . . . I want it all."

It was as if she'd understood every desire, every fantasy he'd had about her. Even the ones that frightened him, those sweet romantic images undeniably more precious now that they were within his reach. With one sweep of her eyes she moved him, bringing life to that emotional void where he'd been numb so long.

"So do I."

Leaning back on her elbows, she dropped her head back in an eloquent act of consent. Moving over her, he touched her as lightly as falling petals from a swollen rose. He ran his fingers down her throat to the delicate hollow, following them with a skimming trail of kisses. Wet and warm, they touched her like raindrops before a summer storm. Giving the same exquisite attention to the rest of her, he steeled himself against the pounding need in his loins. When she began weaving her hips, he moved lower, moistening his lips in her sweet healing wetness. Her breath caught in a ragged gasp, and with one whispery moan she tumbled another one of his walls.

He reached for protection, and together they rolled it on. Striving for one last semblance of control, he managed a breathless smile. "Thunder and lightning?"

Leaning back on the pillows again, she opened her secrets to him like a trusting lover. "Thunder and lightning," she repeated, stroking herself from the valley between her breasts to the nest of auburn curls near the glistening place between her thighs.

He was past words now, intent on following her lead. With a pleasurable shudder, he let her guide him inside her narrow entrance. She contracted around him instantly, urging him deeper into her silken embrace with a tug of his hips and a sizzling sigh. Easing himself halfway to her center, he watched her eyes as the first wave of undiluted pleasure struck her. He'd never held a shooting star, but now he knew what one felt like as her sensuous moves flared to a burning climax around him. Before he could stop it, his guarded well of passion surged forward in a series of hot, hard strokes. Crying her name, he let his last wall tumble as he sank himself into the deepest part of her. She came with him in one stunning explosion of pleasure. The incredible feeling of oneness lingered long after his thundering heartbeat stopped echoing through her body. She lay quietly within his embrace, brushing an occasional kiss to his chest and leaving him to wonder at the miracle of it all.

Later Bryn felt him moving her onto the pillows and covering her with the sheet. Holding her face between his palms, he kissed her several times, each time more beautiful than the last. Lulled by his gentle touch, she couldn't think about anything except their total intimacy and that she wanted it to go on forever.

"Sleep, darling," he whispered, before moving off the bed and heading toward the bathroom.

Drifting in and out of her drowsy state, it took her a moment to realize he'd finished in the bathroom and was out on the deck, securing the doors. She moved around the empty bed trying to find a more comfortable spot. She ended up rolling into the space he'd left. Already cool to the touch, she began nuzzling the sheet, inhaling the scent of their lovemaking in an effort to recreate his presence. Half aroused with wanting him again, she indulged in another new experience, wrapping herself in her lover's scent. Reveling in the hedonistic act, she tugged the material around her and drew the vital fragrance into her body. Nothing, she thought, would ever break the spell of this night.

Rick watched her from the door, enjoying her voluptuous moves as if she'd orchestrated them specifically for him. Moonlight played on the satin curves of her body, tantalizing him with what he saw and what he didn't. The more she nudged herself against the twisted sheet, the more aroused he became. "If I come back to bed, will you wrap your knees around me like that?" he asked.

Tensing at the sound of his voice, she stopped moving on the sheet. Pushing up, she lowered her buttocks to her heels, then looked over her shoulder at him. *Don't stop*, he wanted to tell her, but he knew her private moment had passed and a shared one was about to begin.

"Will you make those sounds for me?" he asked, walking into the room and next to the bed. Bracing his hands on the bed, he leaned in to kiss her hip. "Will you move like that for me?"

When she didn't answer him, he sensed her silence came not from her embarrassment but from her disoriented state. She stared blankly at the dry-cleaning bag he'd taken inside before, and he began to wonder if she'd been aware of what she'd just been doing. Kneeling beside the bed, he began stroking the indentation of her spine.

"Are you really awake?" he asked softly.

"Yes."

"Are you okay?"

"Yes."

"No, you're not," he said, standing quickly to sit beside her. "What's wrong? Did I hurt you before?" Approaching her slowly, he lifted her chin on his fingertips. "Did I scare you? Christ, Bryn, I'm sorry. It's been a while since—"

"Has it?" she asked.

Her question seared the air between them. In the light of a full moon, he could see her eyes narrowing with concern before she lowered her head. "Where did that come from? No, don't turn away," he said, reaching for her shoulder. Relieved that she didn't flinch from his touch, he kissed the warm skin next to his hand. "Not after what we've just been through," he added gently. "Tell me what's bothering you and I'll try to help."

"The other night, after I smeared that pie on your sleeve, I decided I should be the one to take it to the dry cleaner's." She looked away again. "When I was carrying the jacket to the car, I guess I held it close to my face. I smelled perfume on the lapel. Shalimar. I don't wear Shalimar." She plucked at the sheet covering her knee. "Rick, if there's someone else in your life, I have to know, because I can't be with you. I'm not like that and—"

"There's no one else."

"But the perfume—"

"There's no one now. It was over months ago." Shaking his head, he stood up again, suddenly restless. "Do you want to hear this?"

Her palms lay open on her thighs in a gesture of surrender. "I have to hear this."

"Her name is Sharon Burke and she lives on one of the Lower Keys. What we had was a simple, physical relationship."

"Is she a prostitute?"

"No. She'd lost her husband in a boating accident about eight months before we got together. And I was alone too. Bryn, we weren't looking to complicate our lives, but we both had needs, and at the time the idea of an arrangement appeared workable. I suppose the whole affair sounds calculated, and to be honest, it was."

"Did you care for her?"

He hesitated before he began to speak. "I know what you're asking, and all I can say is, I wasn't looking for anything more than what she had to offer." He shrugged at his loss for words. "But situations change. I hadn't called her in several months, and when I finally saw her the other night, she was as ready to call it quits as I was."

"Why?" Bryn asked, twisting around to face him. He came back to the bed. "What happened?"

"You happened," he said, pulling her up on her knees and against him. "And you keep happening. Every time I see you, or touch you or even think about you, I want you."

The power and passion in his voice pushed back other questions she wanted to ask him. Everything about him said his affair was over, and that he wanted her now. Responding to his stirring passion, she accepted his blunt explanation with a hot kiss that brought them both down on the bed. After a valiant struggle to prolong their foreplay, they both scrambled for another packet on the nightstand. When he reached between her thighs and began lifting himself over her, she pushed him back and took the place on top. "Not this time. This time, I want to wrap my knees around you," she whispered, guiding him inside her moist heat. He was hers now, and if she had any lingering doubts, they disappeared in the riveting attention his eyes were paying her. "I want to make those sounds for you when I move on you . . . like this."

Her name formed on his lips, but he was too steeped in pleasure to speak. Sweet torment distorted his mouth until she covered it with a kiss. That she had taken him to his limit so quickly, filled her with a new feminine power and the impulse to use it. Tightening around him, she leaned forward and whispered, "Just like this, Rick." When she heard him gasp, she sank down on his shaft, surrendering them both to a soul-shaking union.

SEVEN

Bryn meant to leave early the next morning but one good-morning kiss led to another, and six A.M. became seven A.M. And then eight A.M. They finally both agreed after a lusty, breathless coupling on his kitchen floor that they had places to go, work that wouldn't wait and problems to solve. But tonight they were definitely reserving for themselves. Yes, tonight made sense, they mumbled through a few more kisses.

Tonight, Bryn silently reminded herself, she was going to ask Rick about things that her grandfather and Liza had attempted to tell her. What did she know about Rick? He was a man of the moment who knew how to push her buttons, and made her take stock of her personal life, especially what she lacked in the man/woman area. Rick Parrish was more than a sexual technician who could bring her to mind-boggling orgasm. His tenderness for her tugged at her heart even now.

Rick kissed her all the way to her car, then pulled her out of it and kicked the door shut to share one last embrace. When he eventually backed away from her, hands in the air, she was still tingling from his touch.

"I have to cancel a reserved charter," he said as much to himself as to her. "I've got paperwork. And there's an engine needing an overhaul." As he started off she didn't bother hiding her frustrated sigh.

"Aw, the hell with it," he said, doing an about-face to close the gap between them. "Tonight's too far away. Meet me at the marina at ten and we'll head down to Key West for the day."

Still heady with their new intimacy, she infused her question with a teasing, breathy innocence. "Is that an order, Captain Parrish?"

She watched him sizing her up with playful exaggeration. He'd never been more relaxed with her. After thoughtfully rubbing his shirtless chest, he rested both hands on his hips. "It is. Are you questioning my authority?"

"Depends on what the punishment is," she said, before biting back a laughter-filled smile. When he made the move to capture her, she blocked him by opening her door and getting in. "I take it back. And besides, I have business in Key West this week and

I can probably get it done today," she said, starting her car.

"If I let you out of my sight long enough," he said with mock gruffness.

"Don't make threats unless you're willing to follow through on them, Captain." Sticking out a lazy tongue, she pulled slowly out of his driveway. "Ten o'clock at the marina."

"I'll be waiting for you."

At five minutes to ten she parked her car at Parrish's Marina. Her heart was racing by the time she got to the roped walkway leading to the docks. When she reached for the thick rope that served as a railing, she hesitated, then brought her hands halfway to her face instead. They were shaking, and she asked herself why the idea of spending the day with him would cause this reaction. But she was kidding herself, because she already knew the real question causing the trembling in her hands and the thumping in her chest. *What was she going to find out about him and his life before she'd met him?*

With a huffy sigh over her fears, she stepped up onto the dock. Rick had already proved himself to be a thoughtful, caring man. And she certainly had no complaints about his powerful sexuality and his ability to reach hers. What kept niggling at her was the rest of him. Sure, he came with character references from virtually everyone on Coconut Key, but his past was a blank. When she felt that sinking sensation in her chest, she squeezed hard on the rope railing. Key West and all its charms were waiting. More important, so was Rick Parrish.

But Rick wasn't waiting alone.

Rick's voice was coming from the other side of the bait shack. "I can't allow her on the boat. Sorry to have to change your plans, but that's always been my policy in this situation."

"Well, no one told us about this policy when we made the reservation two months ago, Captain Parrish. And besides, we asked for Charlie and his boat."

"Charlie works by this marina's rules. If you'll step into the office, we'll credit your charge card in full."

"But I'm barely four months along, and I feel great. If I hadn't mentioned it, you wouldn't have known I'm pregnant. Hey, if I promise not to have the baby until we get back, would you make an—"

Rick cut the woman off before she could end her lighthearted attempt to change his mind. "No exceptions."

As a screaming gull punctuated the tense silence, Bryn found herself pulling for the mother-to-be.

"Come on, honey," her husband said, rattling their fishing poles as he gathered them up with the rest of their gear. "We'll go on to Islamorada."

Grumbling about the "absurd rule," the couple passed Bryn on their way to the office.

"That guy got up on the wrong side of the bed this morning. Better watch yourself with him," the attentive father-to-be said before maneuvering around Bryn, his wife in tow.

By the time the man had finished his warning, Bryn had glued her gaze to Rick. He was standing, hands in the pockets of his khaki shorts, directing his attention away from the couple until he heard the door of the L-shaped building close behind them. Bryn watched him step back as two of his workers passed him on the way to another boat. Their good-natured laughter appeared to rouse him from sobering thoughts, and only then did he notice Bryn. Groping for his sunglasses, which were hanging on a cord around his neck, he shoved them on.

"Been waiting long?"

"Long enough," she answered, feeling the tension pull at her smile. "Practicing safe staring again?" she asked, pointing to his sunglasses. When the question didn't produce a smile, she moved a few steps closer. "Rick, that woman hardly looked pregnant. Is there a Coast Guard regulation or a superstition against pregnant women on boats?"

"No, it's my policy."

"But, I don't—"

"Things are easier this way."

"She didn't look pregnant. I still don't—"

"Captain's orders," he said, draping his arm over her shoulders as he waved off the uncomfortable situation. "So, what have you been doing with yourself for the last couple of hours?"

There was no doubt in her mind that he didn't want to talk about the uncomfortable situation that had occurred minutes earlier. By rights she had to let it go, too, even if there was more to the story. Marina policy was in Rick's domain and none of her business. "What have I been doing with myself? Making phone calls. You know, it's amazing how much work I can accomplish with a phone and a fax machine from right here in the Keys. People fax everything these days."

Rick guided her toward his Jeep. "Tell me about it," he said, as he dropped a kiss to her cheek.

"The price list for Italian milk-glass light fixtures? The long-awaited decision on the drapery pattern about to be hung in all the Smithdale Inns nationwide?" she asked, ruffling the caramel-colored hair on his arm. "Oh, no. We have much more interesting subjects to talk about."

"True. If we don't get moving on this fund-raiser, we'll be scrambling around with Kool-Aid stands and dog-bathing services to pay for that ambulance," he said as he watched her get into the Jeep. He walked around the vehicle, pausing to look at the car the couple had come in.

As she waited for him to get in, Bryn had to admit that he was right. They had committed themselves to a community project, and she finally had a specific idea to talk over with him. Still, she couldn't pretend she wasn't disappointed when he didn't take her hint to talk about themselves. Or, more to the point, about himself.

"So, have you come up with that pizzazzy idea you threatened me with, or should we shoot for the fishing tournament?"

"I do have an idea. You know, I run in the morning and—" She broke off to squint at him. "Why are you smiling?"

"I know you run in the morning. I see you over there by that jacaranda tree doing your warm-up."

"You've been watching me?"

"Bryn Madison, does it surprise you to know that I haven't been able to keep my eyes off you? I've developed an acute affinity for your red running shorts," he said, starting the Jeep and shifting into reverse. "I like them almost as much as the black satin pair."

"They're nylon," she said, trying to remove the smile from her face. With his head still tilted in her direction and his grin still teasing her, she looked straight ahead. "I was thinking about a five-day sports festival topped off with a 10K fun run. There'd be an activity for everyone. One day for handicapped, another for children, one for the over-sixty group. Different events for every day."

He lifted his foot off the clutch and eased out of his parking space. "Go on, I'm listening."

"Liza has a list of potential sponsors. They'll probably like the idea of a week-long event because they'll be advertising their name to a different crowd each day."

"True," he said, nodding, deep in thought. "I know the manager of a radio station in Key West, and he'll publicize anything for a good cause. You know, I think you've got something here." Driving out of the parking lot, he headed for the highway. "Keep talking."

Pulling her knee up, she shifted in her seat, and for the next forty-five minutes they worked out more details.

"What's your business in Key West today?" he asked as he pulled into a tree-shaded parking spot just off Duval Street.

Shoving her hair out of her face, she climbed out of the Jeep and into his arms. "I have to tell a man named Louis Trudeaux that I won't be needing him as a chef for Chez Madison. He doesn't have a phone, but he assured me I can usually find him at Sloppy Joe's."

"You're doing pretty well with this idea of changing the restaurant back to Pappy's Crab Shack, aren't you?"

"Yes, I am, Rick. I want what's best for my grandfather."

"You really care about that old guy, don't you?"

Closing her eyes, she dropped her forehead against Rick's chest. All morning long she'd worried about getting Rick to reveal his past, but when the tables were turned, she didn't find it easy herself. "Shouldn't every little girl love her grandfather and want to show it now and then?"

"I guess so," he said, lifting her chin on one finger and giving her a peculiar look. "Come on, let's do this town."

Strolling along Duval Street, she was content to weave in and out of the pedestrian traffic with Rick by her side. When they came across a Rastafarian street rapper making up songs about the people walking by him, they stopped to listen to his pleasantly naughty lyrics. A small crowd gathered, and between songs a little boy squirmed between them, calling for his daddy.

Bryn managed to stoop down in the crowd. "Are you lost?"

"No," he said, moving away from Bryn's hand, then tugging on the hem of Rick's shorts. "I want Daddy to pick me up."

Bryn raised her head to look at Rick. His face went blank and he looked mildly shocked. Bryn swallowed as she looked from his face to the chubby fingers clenched near his knees. The towheaded child had his cheek pressed against Rick's leg.

"I want to see the music, Daddy."

Bryn slowly stood up, not daring to meet Rick's growing expression of astonishment. He had a child. A beautiful child he'd never mentioned to her. A beautiful child he wasn't touching or talking to or acknowledging in any way. How could she have been so stupid not to have listened to Liza or her grandfather when they offered to tell her about his past? The moment suddenly ended when another man wormed his way through the knot of people and picked up the boy.

"Sorry," he said, "but they get away from you fast in a crowd like this. Brandon must have thought you were me," he said to Rick as he chucked his son under the chin. "Right, son?"

The child pointed an accusing finger at Rick. "He's not my daddy."

"Must have been the khaki shorts," the man said, referring to the nearly identical pairs Rick and he wore. When Rick didn't reply, the man turned his attention to Bryn. "Must have been the khaki shorts," he said again, before disappearing into the crowd with his son.

Pressing her fingers between her breasts, she laughed nervously. "Rick, for a crazy moment I thought that he was yours."

"No kids. Let's go," he said, as he regained his color. Guiding her to an emptier part of the sidewalk, his words rushed out. "About the Crab Shack. I liked your idea about a piano. Tweed MacNeil plays piano, and Pappy already has him over with his guitar."

"Wait a minute," she insisted, stopping in the middle of the sidewalk. Several people walked around them as Rick waited for what Bryn would say or do next. She struggled in painful silence for all of two seconds.

"Do you realize how little I know about you? I mean other than the consensus that you're Coconut Key's resident hero."

"There's nothing much to know. What you see is what you get." He reached for her hand, but she folded her arms across her middle. "Come on, Bryn, I think I know where there's a used piano for sale."

"You're avoiding talking about yourself. Why? What have you done? Lost a fortune at the dog track? Killed your wife? Spent time in prison?" With each question, she moved closer to him. With each question, he seemed further away.

"Hey, we're holding up traffic," he said, fixing a furtive gaze toward a person moving around them.

She let him take her hand and guide her around the corner. Standing beside her, he dropped his shoulder against a high white wall embedded with conch shells and gave her a tight-lipped smile.

Was she pushing? Was there much to know? Looking around at the pastel houses and the easygoing atmosphere, she wondered if she was approaching this all wrong. As curious as she was, she wasn't going to learn anything worth knowing by prying. Then again, if this relationship was worth anything to him, he had to talk to her. And he had to do it now, or she knew the last twenty hours had all been a mistake. She held her breath until little stars scattered over her field of vision.

Raising his finger, he stroked her nose. "I was married. I'm not anymore. I don't have kids. I do have a master's degree in marine biology. I'm staying in the Keys until a hurricane takes me. And as far as being anyone's local hero, it's news to me. If that's all you need to know, then can we get on with this day?"

She knew she ought to be grateful that he'd told her that much, but something compelled her to try one more time. "Rick, that reads like a laundry list. When I asked you about your past—"

"Operative word there, Bryn, is *past*. I have to tell you that my past now extends back to last night when you seduced me. I think we burned out a few brain cells."

"I seduced you?" She laughed, pressing both hands to her chest.

"And compromised my good name. Yes, ma'am, you did," he said, leaning his back against the wall as he pulled her to stand between his legs. His hair-roughened legs tickled against the satiny smoothness of hers. "Look, why don't you go on down to Sloppy Joe's and break the news to your chef. Meanwhile, I'm heading up those stairs across the street to Wigglin' Willie's office."

"Who?"

"Wigglin' Willie, the deejay. He does the radio commercials for my fishing charters. I'm going to discuss the Coconut Key Sports Festival with him."

"But we don't have anything firmed up yet."

Cuddling her closer, he rested his chin on her head and whispered, "Firmed up, is that what you said? Girl, you've got to stop talking sexy like that."

"Or what?" she asked, bracing herself with one hand against his flat, hard stomach. Warm sensations were already curling their way through her belly. Breathing in the fresh scents of his cotton shirt, the sea breeze, and his maleness, she bunched the material in her fist and closed her eyes.

Nipping at her earlobe with the edges of his teeth, he stopped long enough to whisper, "Or I swear I'll take you against this wall."

He'd caught her off guard, and for one extraordinary instant the rest of the world fell away, leaving her holding her breath again as her mind filled with the erotic images he'd suggested. When he stopped doing that incredible thing to her ear, she opened her eyes to his. Before she could lower her lashes, the purring had started low in her belly.

"You've never . . . ?" he began asking.

Fighting back a startled smile, she shook her head. With her fingers pressed against his chest, she could feel his strengthening heartbeat. "I haven't done a lot of things."

His response left her weak-kneed and wanting.

"You will."

Her reply shocked her. "When?"

Dropping his head back against the wall, he let loose with a stream of curses, letting them roll under his breath until he could form a coherent sentence.

"Whenever you want."

Want? It wasn't a matter of want anymore. She craved him, craved his touch and the way he moved on her and in her. Craved the desperate sounds he made when nothing existed except the heat of their embrace. Craved the tenderness he lavished on her. When was it going to stop? She ran her fingers down his arms, circling his wrist to bring his hand to her lips. "Rick, I can't believe how you make me feel," she whispered. "No one has ever done this to me before. You look at me and all I want to do is get closer." The desperate excitement of her own words alarmed her, and she wondered what Rick was hearing between the lines. Making a funny face at him, she bantered her way out of the drama. "Captain Parrish, what are you doing to me?"

What are you doing to me? Rick thought to himself. Resting his forehead against hers, he waited for a man walking a cat on a leash to pass them. Bryn was talking about something far more compelling than their wild rides through heaven and hell. He could deal with this; all he had to do was remember she wasn't going to be around forever. That Pappy's Crab Shack was coming back. And that he'd lived without a commitment or a plan for the last five years. Meanwhile, they had time and he wasn't going to waste a second of it.

"Bryn, let's not go back to Coconut Key tonight. I know a guest house over on White Street. We'll get a room there and go back tomorrow." When she hesitated, he slipped his hands around her waist, molded her against him and whispered hotly against her ear. "We'll come back to this spot about three o'clock in the morning and I'll make good on my promise," he said, taking one of her hands and pressing it flat against the wall by his hip. "What do you say?" he asked, daring her as much with his question as with his devilish expression.

"Are you serious?"

"No, but I had you—ouch!" He dodged her playful blow before catching her hands and twisting her around into his embrace. "I'm serious about staying over. We could take in the sunset at Mallory Square, and I'll let you read the menu to me at this French restaurant I know. How does that sound?"

"It sounds wonderful. I'll call my grandfather with the phone number of where we're staying. We would make it back early tomorrow, wouldn't we? I want to see him using his walker."

"Any time you say."

"Then my answer's yes."

"All right," he said, kissing her soundly. "I'll look up the number of that guest house and give them a call from Willie's."

"Did you mean it about having him start making announcements about the fund-raiser? Shouldn't we clear this idea with someone first?"

"No. There's one thing about Liza you ought to know. When she delegates authority, she expects you to act on it. We're the cochair-whatevers, and we've agreed it's a good idea. So let's go for it. Wigglin' Willie can start talking it up without every detail in place, which will put us ahead that much more. I'll meet you at Sloppy Joe's in about an hour."

Rick found her at Sloppy Joe's sitting on a bar stool surrounded by three Ernest Hemingway look-alikes. Watching her clinking glasses with the three charmers made him smile. Everything about her had relaxed since she'd come to the Keys. Enjoying his view of her, he reviewed the outer changes. With each move she made, her curls jiggled and bounced around her head, inviting his touch. The buttoned suits and high heels were replaced with shorts and matching tops, or the flirty little lime-colored sundress with the spaghetti straps that she wore today.

Moving into a shadowy corner, he reminded himself that he had to be careful around her. Once Bryn got *him* started talking, he'd tell her about Angie, and that would trigger all the old pain he kept buried. He had no doubt she could do it too. She'd opened him up last night and brought out feelings and passions he thought were dead. Experiencing her on that level of intimacy had turned out to be phenomenal, but he had to stop there. And whatever she had to tell him about herself, well . . . he wasn't so sure he wanted to hear it. All he wanted, he reminded himself firmly, was a few weeks to bask in her womanly warmth. After that his world could spin on without her. This feeling of being dazzled by her, consumed with wanting her, would pass. It had to pass. He'd make it pass, dammit.

Making his way to a table near her bar stool, he told himself he could wait patiently for her to notice him. He ordered a rum and Coke while someone fiddled with a portable radio between music sets. While Rick watched her out of the corner of his eye, Jimmy Buffet's "Why Don't We Get Drunk And Screw?" started playing. After a spontaneous sing-along, one of the men pulled a paperback from his back pocket and began reading to her. She appeared to be listening attentively, but Rick saw her glance over the man's shoulder once or twice. Christ, was the guy going to bore her to death by reading another entire page from *Islands in the Stream*? Rick drummed his fingers on the table. She probably needed rescuing, and he might as well be the one. Scooting back his chair, he walked into her line of vision. The smile that exploded on her face hit him in the stomach with the force of a hurricane.

One man poked the reader in the side, and as his voice trailed off, the sea of Hemingways parted for Rick.

"Hi."

"Hi."

A chorus of soft chuckles enveloped the two of them before the bearded men drifted away.

He was not going to make a romantic fool of himself. Standing a conservative ten inches away from her, he handed her a paper with a phone number written on it, saying, "We have a room at Lord Eddie's. It overlooks a walled garden and a pool filled with monster goldfish. Breakfast will be croissants, French roast coffee, papaya, and fresh-squeezed orange juice. Think you can survive on that?"

Reaching out to him, she smoothed back his hair, then rested her hand on his shoulder. "I'm not sure. I need to know one more thing," she said.

"What?"

"How big is the bed?"

Closing his eyes, he took a step forward and slumped into her arms with a groan. "Big enough," he managed to tell her between fits of laughter. "And if it's not, there's always that wall off Duval Street."

She left him laughing, saying, "I'm calling my grandfather. He should be awake from his nap."

Taking her seat at the bar, Rick watched her walk away as he sipped his drink. Once she returned, he would ask her how her meeting with the chef had gone. Then he'd take her to Olivia Street to check out the piano for sale. Resting his elbows on the bar, he thought about Pappy's Crab Shack and how great it would be having it back again. True, it wouldn't be exactly like old times, but he could learn to live with it, he supposed. That god-awful banana yellow had to go though, and somehow he'd locate an artist to re-create the mermaid. This evening over dinner he'd discuss it all with Bryn.

Just as he turned toward the bartender to order another drink, Bryn's hands closed around his wrist. He looked up from her icy grip to see her eyes filled with tears.

"Rick, we have to leave. Now," she said in a choked voice.

"What's happened?"

"My grandfather was trying out his walker on his own and fell and hit his head. They haven't been able to bring him around. Rick, I'm scared."

His arms were around her before he could speak. "It's going to be okay," he said. "I'll be with you."

"Bryn, you've got to calm down. They said he was only out for fifteen minutes."

Her hands came down from her face to gesture wildly. "Well, how long does it take to X-ray someone's head? And why can't I go downstairs to wait for him?"

He knew by now she wasn't expecting answers from him. She'd become more frantic with each passing mile on their way back from Key West. All he could do was reassure her, and that wasn't calming her at all. He had to try. Shrugging his shoulders, he reached for her again.

"No," she said, shaking her head as she pushed off the wall in the little blue alcove. Holding up her hands, she motioned for him to move away. "I don't deserve a hug at the moment."

"What? What are you talking about?" he asked, watching her closely. Seeing her first tears fall, his heart felt as if it were crimping around the edges. "Bryn, please," he begged, "what is it?"

"It's me," she whispered hoarsely. "I needed to tell him something." Rubbing her eyes, she stood tall, continuing to keep her distance from Rick. "Maybe it's too late."

"He's going to be fine. Come on, Bryn. What are we talking about here? Pappy knows you love him, and he loves you. Do you know what he once told me about you? 'She's a pistol.'" When that didn't raise a smile, he took her by the elbows and made her look at him. "So what is it? You never got around to explaining why you took ten cents off his dresser when you were seven years old? You washed the car with his good white shirt?" He gave her a tiny shake. "You don't have to apologize. That old man thinks the world of you. So whatever absolution you think you need to ask for, isn't important."

"It's none of those things, Rick."

"Go on. Don't stop now," he said, loosening his grip.

"I have to tell him that I forgive him. I should have told him the moment I found out the truth." Looking away, she slowly shook her head. "But I didn't, I didn't."

Rick led her to a sofa and sat down beside her. Reaching for a tissue, he fumbled, pulling out a handful instead, and shoved them into her hands. At least that elicited a snorted laugh from her. After a while she stopped dabbing her eyes and looked up at him.

"How much do you know about my grandfather's life before he came to the Keys?"

He started to speak, but realized he had virtually nothing to say. "Bryn, people down here leave a person's past alone. They don't ask questions about a newcomer's background either. What I know about Pappy's past can fit in a thimble. It's what I know about him now that counts. He's a good man."

"I know that. But what you don't know is, he had a fight with his brother, my uncle Ron, over the family business. Uncle Ron wanted him to open up another auto parts store in the next county, but Grandfather refused. Everyone in the family had an opinion about it, even my grandmother. She pushed and pushed for him to open another store." Bryn stopped talking, staring hard into the hallway. Finally she sighed and leaned back against the sofa. "One day, after about a month of this, Grandfather suddenly packed a suitcase and left town."

Rick twisted slowly around to look at her. "He left your grandmother?"

Bryn nodded. "We couldn't figure it out. Grandmother refused to talk about it. She said it was too humiliating. Within a year they were divorced and he'd started his life over down here. A few years later everyone praised Uncle Ron for marrying her. My father was so angry with Grandfather that he wouldn't let us mention his name." Tears started down her face again. "For years I almost forgot about him— forgot this wonderful man who always treated me like a princess."

"What happened?"

"After my grandmother and Uncle Ron died in a car accident, we were going through her things. I found a stack of love letters."

"Ah, from Pappy," Rick said, reaching for her hand.

She gulped and swallowed. "From my uncle Ron. They were seeing each other during her marriage to my grandfather. Rick, she was having an affair with his brother, and he must have found out about it. His pride and his stubborn streak kept us apart."

"But you've been coming to see him, Bryn."

Swiping at her nose with the ball of tissues, she said, "Only after I'd read those letters. I think he knows that I know about his brother and my grandmother. Rick, I should have said something to him."

"Oh, Bryn," he said, shifting uneasily. "Why do you want to bring up something that painful from the past? Why not let it alone?"

"And pretend nothing ever happened? Oh no, this kind of hurt, going on as long as it has, needs its moment in the light. I've already told him how badly I feel about missing all those years with him, but I never told him I've forgiven him for not being there, and for his pretending we all stopped existing when he found out about Uncle Ron and my grandmother." Picking at the ball of tissue, she asked in a desperate whisper, "Don't you see?"

"I see that an old man who has the granddaughter he adores with him doesn't need to be reminded about a miserable time from his past. Bryn, I'd reconsider telling him." He watched for a sign that he'd made his point, but she continued to cry and he wasn't certain how to read a woman's tears anymore. It had been so long. . . . Pinching the bridge of his nose, he said, "If you still feel compelled, I'd highly recommend you don't tell him until he's back on his feet."

Staring hard again into the hall, she shook her head in confusion. "I'm not sure what to do. I have to think." Raising her hands in a helpless gesture, she thumped them against her chest. "Rick, you don't ever know when people you love are going to leave you."

"I know, I know," he said, pulling her into his arms when she hid her face in her hands. Patting her back, he whispered words of comfort as he thought about Pappy. And Angie. If he waited long enough, he reassured himself, all those chaotic thoughts trying to claim him would drift to the back of his mind. Pulling her closer, he pressed a kiss against the curly top of her head.

"Excuse me," came a voice from the hallway. "Pappy Madison is back in his room."

Bryn sat up, clutching the raggedy remnants of tissues to her breast. "Is he going to be okay?"

"No broken bones. At least in his skull. We should have known Pappy would be too hardheaded. He's going to be fine."

"Can we see him?" Bryn asked as Rick stood up with her.

"The nurse will be out to get you in a minute."

"Thank you, Doctor," she said, slipping her arms around Rick's waist. As the doctor walked away she looked up at Rick. "Thank you for being here. And for listening. I think I would have really lost it if you hadn't been here for me."

Brushing her hair away from her brow, he stared down into her eyes and smiled. He didn't agree with the way she wanted to handle things with Pappy, but at least she'd heard him out. Maybe those scenes from his past would stop replaying and he could start this afternoon in the present with Bryn again.

"Hey," he said, thumbing away the moisture below her eyes, "you almost lost it last time we stood in this alcove too. Remember?"

Her sigh was a cleansing one, deep and revitalizing. "What I remember most is that you almost kissed me. Or did I almost kiss you?"

Pulling her close, he brushed his lips against hers in a sweet kiss. "Go ahead, blame it on me," he said, happy to have made another memory to add to his list.

EIGHT

"That's it," Bryn said, standing in the middle of Pappy's Crab Shack. Pointing to the second smear of paint on the wall, she nodded confidently to the group as the reinstalled jukebox played another oldie. "This, uh," she began, then paused to look at the paint chip card in her hand, "Sumatra Tan is so much more workable than Bark Beige or Café au Lait. You see, there's not as much gray . . ." she said, squinting at the wall and then the paint chip card. "At least, I don't think—"

"Quick," Rick said to the rest of the people in the room, "start rolling it on before she changes her mind."

"Ha-ha. Very funny," she said good-naturedly amid their laughing. Walking over to the far end of the bar, she heard Rick coming up behind her. Slapping the paint chips onto the refinished wood surface, she turned to point at him.

"Just because I've decided to get back to basics with the decor doesn't mean I'm willing to settle for second best for Pappy's Crab Shack."

In the only shadowed corner of the room, Rick took her finger between his teeth, sucked it into his mouth, and swirled his tongue around it. For one intense second she thought she was going to embarrass herself by gasping out loud. Then he released her finger and turned back toward the rest of the people.

"Bryn's right, Captain Parrish," Rita Small said, from her place by the secondhand piano. Chiseling off suspiciously barnaclelike substances from the top, she stopped long enough to offer her opinion. "This old place is going to be as comfy as before, only fresher. Pappy's going to love what Bryn's done to the place."

"How's his head from that fall he had?" Jiggy asked.

"Harder than ever," Rick said as he went down the stairs. "I'm going for that extra tarp in the truck."

"Need help with it?" Jiggy asked.

"No, thanks. Just keep stirring that paint and I'll be up with it in a minute."

"Okay," Jiggy said, before turning his attention to Bryn. "Now that Pappy's started his physical therapy, when will he be well enough to have a look at the place?"

"The doctor says the week of the sports festival is the soonest we can have him back. I'll never be able to thank you all enough for pitching in with this," she said, raising her hands to indicate the interior of the Crab Shack. "With so much going on with the festival, Grandfather's hospital stay, my own business, and then turning this restaurant project around, I don't know how I'd have managed without you."

Liza Manning looked up from the papers spread out before her on the opposite end of the bar. "Seems only right that we should, since Pappy insisted we use the place as headquarters during Sports Festival Week. Besides, what are friends for?"

"Ms. Manning, don't go getting all sappy or I'll cry in this paint and mess it up," Jiggy said from his squatting position next to a paint can. Lifting the stir stick, he let the rich tan liquid dribble off the end. "Looks like the color of the sand over on August Moon Key."

Bryn glanced away from the old brass clock she had started polishing to glimpse the color. Smiling, she turned back to the clock again, recalling the afternoon a few days ago when Rick helped her pick it out in an antique shop in Key West. That was the same day he'd finally gotten to show her the second-hand piano Rita was working on. The same day they'd finally checked into Lord Eddie's and made love all afternoon. "August Moon Key," she said slowly. "That sounds so romantic."

"Captain Parrish used to think so," Jiggy said as he concentrated on neatly pouring the paint from the can into the paint tray. "He used to take Angie there every chance he could."

The room went silent, leaving Bryn with the deafening sound of her pounding heart.

"Hush up, Jiggy, or I'll put a tangle in your tackle so tight that you'll go blind getting it straight again," Liza said.

Rita Small thunked the chisel onto the piano and noisily cleared her throat before reaching for the sandpaper by her feet. "Liza, I believe you've been spending too much time with Pappy."

Rita's words of admonishment came a few seconds too late to ring true. Eight pairs of eyes were now slowly turning toward Bryn. Heat crept up her face, making her skin sting. Why should it matter to her if Rick used to take his wife to a deserted little island? That happened years ago; they were divorced now and that's what mattered. Shoving a lock of hair away from one eyebrow, she found herself wondering once again why Rick never mentioned his ex-wife.

If Angie Parrish was no longer a part of his life, then why hadn't he brought her up in the normal course of their conversations? Had Angie been the dragon lady who broke Rick's heart? Or did Rick continue to feel guilty because he had been the cause of their divorce? He'd had no trouble explaining Sharon Burke to her. Why not his ex-wife? Was he still in love with her?

Squeezing her eyes shut, Bryn tried desperately to get control of her wandering thoughts. Until her grandfather was safely on both feet again, the rest of her life was on hold anyway. Whatever the explanation for Rick's continued silence, she was crazy to allow herself to be torn apart like this. She fought to stay in control of her thoughts as they raced ahead unchecked. These feelings for Rick existed in a world apart from the rest of her life, and because of that, she could handle them. Besides, what good would it do for her to force him to talk about his past? She'd already tried several times anyway. What they were sharing had nothing to do with the past, and who cared about the future? The answer to that brash question left her breathless. *She* cared about the future, because she was in love with Rick Parrish.

Admitting to herself what she'd been suspecting for days, had her shaking all over. Pressing the back of her hand over her lips, she pulled in a deep breath through her nostrils, then let it out slowly. This summer on Coconut Key was about more than taking care of her grandfather. For the first time in her life she was taking care of her own needs. She had happily put the rest of her life on hold, except the part of her that filled with joy each time Rick walked in the room, the same part that died a little each time he left. Now that she'd admitted to herself that she was in love with Rick, it all made sense. So why wasn't she happier about the revelation?

With the disquieting whispers going on around her, she slid onto a bar stool with a sigh and stared out at Marina Road. When it came to the subject of Rick's past, she spent more time excusing his silence then truly ignoring it. Sooner or later she was going to have to confront Rick about it, because the simplicity of their togetherness had begun dissolving in a sea of unanswered questions. All the lighthearted laughter, comfortable companionship, and steamy sex weren't going to be enough to keep Bryn's fear at bay much longer. Especially since the object of that fear had been named. Angie Parrish.

Bryn sensed the rest of the committee and the several volunteers behind her still reacting to the mention of Angie with murmers punctuated by silence. This miserable situation couldn't last forever, she told herself. It didn't.

Rick walked into the room with the rolled-up tarp balanced over one of his muscular shoulders. He winked at her, and for one glorious instant the tension within her melted into a pulsing mass of pleasure. Angie who? she thought flippantly.

"You must have been talking about me, because you all look as guilty as sin," he said, letting the tarp slam onto the floor. "What's up?"

Meek little Hazel Miller astonished Bryn with her reply. "Why, Captain Parrish, I was thinking about a community fish barbecue to wind up the festival week." Pointing over the railing, she added, "Right down there in the palm grove. What do you think?"

"Sounds like a great idea, but I've got to run it by the other chair. Bryn?"

This was her moment to prove to all of them that she'd been unaffected by the mention of Rick's ex-wife. Besides that, she had an idea to wind up the fund-raising event. Smiling, she turned to face the group. "Hazel, that sounds like fun. I have another idea that, I think, we could combine with yours, but I want to work on it with Rick before I bring it up for a vote."

Casting a slow glance toward him, she lowered her lashes in a private invitation he had become intimately acquainted with over the last week. He puffed out his cheeks, then blew softly through his lips.

"I'll give a listen, Bryn," he said, before turning his attention to unrolling the tarp and draping it over the far end of the bar.

If she knew Rick Parrish, he was going to approve of her idea with gusto. Picturing the private presentation she planned for Rick, she leaned forward on her elbows and smiled to herself. Just a few more hours and she'd have him alone.

"Can I turn around now and have a look?" Rick asked, scratching the bridge of his nose under the blindfold. Straddling a chair in the middle of his living room, he leaned his head back. "Bryn?"

"No. You promised not to look until I tell you it's okay to remove it. And I'll be . . . oops!"

Something clattered to the parquet floor behind him. Running his tongue along the inside of his cheek, he lowered his chin to his stacked fists on the back of the chair. "You brought props along for your, uh, presentation?"

"A few."

"Are you sure you want to go to all this trouble to convince me that this idea, whatever it is, is better than Hazel Miller's plain old fish barbecue?" Lifting his chin from the back of his hands, he started to twist around. "Bryn?"

"I'm over here," she said, close to his ear.

Her sultry voice sent a shiver of anticipation down his spine. Cocking his chin, he reached for his blindfold. "Now?"

"Not yet," she said, trailing something cool and smooth across his cheek. Her cinnamony scent invaded his nostrils, stirring his libido with familiar grace. Suddenly she was on the other side of him, close to his other ear.

"I'll tell you when, Captain Parrish," she said, before nipping his ear.

"Ouch!" he managed, reaching out in a blind grab for her. Missing her, he tried again and almost fell off the chair. Perhaps surrender would be the better part of victory. And he might maintain a shred of dignity along the way. "This is getting kinky."

"To each his own fantasies," she said, dragging what he now suspected was a piece of satin, wrapped around her fingers, below the hems of his shorts.

Squirming on the chair, he said playfully, "Well, in that case, want to tie my hands?"

"Rick!"

"Okay, okay. Want me to tie your hands?"

"Why don't you just take off that blindfold?"

Loosening the bandanna with a few tugs, he pulled it down around his neck and stared. "Cripes," was all he could manage.

Standing before him, with her bare feet spread apart, she was bracing both gloved hands on a shiny lacquered cane planted squarely on the floor between her feet. She wiggled her painted red toenails as his gaze skated up her long, tan legs. Black satiny running shorts snagged his attention for a full five seconds before his gaze meandered on to her white satin vest with the pearl studs.

Rick swallowed. Her matching white satin gloves only served to accentuate her daringly exposed flesh. "Where's your blouse?" he asked after moving his gaze back down the neckline that plunged halfway to her navel.

"In your bedroom." Shifting her weight from one foot to the other, she pulled her top hat low over her brow. Tracing her red bow tie with a fingertip, she asked, "Well, what do you think?"

He started to rise from the chair. "Think? I think all the blood has left my brain and gone south."

"Down, darling. I mean, what do you think about my compromise?"

"Compromise," he murmured, totally mesmerized by her sexy costume. "I can be compromised."

"Rick, this is my idea of semiformal ball attire. I thought about a banquet or maybe a formal dinner dance." She took a step closer to his chair. "But I want a memorable affair, something different to make this fund-raiser stand out from all the rest. Past or future."

When she cupped his chin with one gloved hand, Rick recognized the smooth cool feel of the satin she'd teased him with when he was blindfolded. Now that he could see her doing it, the resulting physical response was the same—he was squirming again.

"I thought a combination of ideas might catch your interest. You see? From the waist up, everyone has to wear formal attire, but everything below the waist, in keeping with the sports theme, has to be sports clothing of some sort." Tapping her cane on the leg of his chair, she asked, "What do you think? Could people have fun with this?"

"I'll have to see," he said, standing up and tugging off his T-shirt. "Are you naked under that?"

Glancing down at her breasts, she said, "Well, of course I'm naked under this. Everyone's naked under their clothes." Exchanging her next sentence for a scream, she made a run for it when he began chasing her around the coffee table. "What are you doing?" she asked, her cane clattering to the floor again as she sprinted for the dining room.

"Practicing for the 10K obstacle course." Once he had her trapped against the dining room credenza, he lifted her up in his arms, announcing, "I win!" Nuzzling her cleavage, he set her on the edge of the credenza and unbuttoned her vest. "And now I claim my prize," he said, covering the tip of one breast with his mouth. Her tightly beaded nipple fit against the curve of his tongue like a pink pearl inside an oyster. After a moment he tasted the other one, giving it the same delicious attention before lifting his head to see her reaction.

Leaning back on one hand, she lifted her gaze to his as she skimmed her fingertips between her breasts. "What do you think of my hybrid concept now that you've explored it?"

Raising his eyebrows, he continued his meticulous perusal. "Pretty pizzazzy."

"But are you thoroughly convinced that this is the best idea?" she asked with a teasing wink.

"Not quite yet," he said, taking off her hat and tossing it over his shoulder.

"What can I do to convince you, Captain Parrish?"

"Hold on a second and I'll let you know," he said, trailing kisses down her throat and onto her breast again. He felt her hand, encased in white satin, sliding over his shoulder, pulling him closer as she dropped her head back.

"Don't wait too long," she said in a husky whisper.

"For starters, I'm convinced I like the taste of your formal half," he said, pushing her vest back to press kisses across the tops of her breasts. When she began shrugging her shoulders to slip out of her vest, he helped her pull it off. Reaching for her bow tie, he studied it a moment, then decided to leave it, not wanting to explore the reason why. All he knew was that she'd put it on for him and, combined with the rest of the outfit she was half wearing, it excited the hell out of him. Running his fingers down her front, he captured her breasts, thumbing her nipples with exquisite care. He loved the way they stiffened with only a look from him, but the way they felt against his fingers and mouth was magical. Pretending seriousness, he asked, "So you're convinced that this formal half combined with this informal half will work together well?"

"Perhaps we should experiment and see," she said, inserting a gloved finger between his lips. When he caught a piece of satin between his teeth, she began working her hand out of the glove. In an agonizingly slow minute she managed to peel the white satin down her arm and withdraw her hand while he kept the glove in his mouth. Lifting her off the credenza, he turned toward the bedroom.

"Not the bed. This is starting to feel like more of a floor experiment," she said, taking the glove from his mouth and motioning toward the rug nearby. They were both out of their shorts and kneeling face to face in a matter of seconds.

"Your experiment or mine?" he asked, after a long hot look from the nest of auburn curls at the apex of her thighs to the bright red lipstick still coloring her lips.

"Mine," she said, pushing him back on the rug. Picking up the glove she'd dropped, she dragged it down his naked body until she produced the effect she wanted.

Tossing it aside, she drew her gloved fingers over him, stroking him boldly. When she heard the hiss of air being sucked between his teeth, she changed hands, gentling her touch as her skin met his. "I think this combination is having a satisfactory effect," she said in a breathy whisper.

"Uh, I think this is moving out of the realm of satisfactory and into something spectacular."

"You appear to have the evidence to support that theory, Captain." When he didn't have a quick retort, she continued. "Isn't compromise wonderful? A little something from me, a little something from you, and before you know it," she said, bending low to run her lips across his flat, hard stomach, "everyone's having a wonderful time. What do you think, Rick?"

Pushing up on one elbow, he rolled her onto her back, covering her mouth with a long, slow kiss. He raised his head enough to speak. "I think I can better answer that question once I find out what the informal half of you tastes like," he said as he lowered his mouth to her navel and then below.

He watched her from his deck a week later as she transplanted petunias into the planter near the bottom of the stairs. Over the past few days she'd become quieter. At first he thought it was the relaxed feeling between them that didn't demand a constant stream of conversation, but her reflective mood had begun to worry him. If he didn't know better, he'd think she was withdrawing from him. But he did know better. Every night they became closer in their profound physical intimacy. Walking down the stairs, he sat on the second step from the bottom. "I thought Rita was going to leave the meeting the other night to run home and start putting together her outfit for the ball."

Scratching the soil with the three-prong gardening tool, Bryn nodded. "Everyone thought the idea sounded like fun. By the way, Liza called to ask if you'd get in touch with Wigglin' Willie to add the ball to his announcements."

"I already took care of that."

An anxious silence hung between them, at least he felt anxious with it. Leaning back on his elbows, he rested an ankle on his knee. "That planter hasn't had flowers in it in years," he said.

Bryn stopped loosening the soil and propped her wrist on the edge of the curved terra-cotta container. "I, uh, had to do something with those petunias lining the walkway to the Crab Shack. There are enough here to fill the two containers on your deck."

"All red ones?"

"Yes, is that okay?" she asked, pushing back the royal blue broad-brimmed straw hat to brush perspiration from her brow.

"I wouldn't let you plant them if they weren't red," he said teasingly.

"Why not?" she asked, reaching for a flowering plant from the flat next to her knees.

He studied her as prickles started down his spine. Even in their earliest encounters, she'd never sounded as stilted as she did now.

Dropping his foot to the bottom step, he leaned forward to rest his arms on his thighs. Maybe he was the one having a strange morning. Time was speeding by; the sports festival was a week away. Pappy would be well enough to come home for it, and that meant Bryn's time on Coconut Key was coming to an end. Rubbing his eyes, he reminded himself that he was the man he was today because of self-discipline. Looking up at her, he said gently, "I'll always associate the color red with you."

Patting the soil around the petunia, she lifted the small watering can, splashing a generous amount at the base of the plant. "I'm driving up to Key Largo today," she said, ignoring what he'd said. "Some people by the name of Dixon want their pool cabana redecorated." Muddy water spilled over the edge and onto her thighs. "Damn," she muttered, smearing the spill as she tried to brush it off.

"Here," Rick said, jumping to his feet and taking the watering can from her hand. "I'll rinse you off."

"Don't. Please don't, I can do it myself."

Relinquishing the can to her, he sank back onto the step. "What's wrong?"

"What's wrong? I just made a mess, that's all," she said with an exaggerated shrug.

"I'm not talking about that and you know it," he said quietly as he stood, then helped her to her feet. "Come on, Bryn, where's that easy flow between us? What's happened? Is it Pappy again?" That had to be it. "Bryn, I'm sorry. I've been so wrapped up in my work and the sports festival, I never asked you how that conversation went with you and Pappy."

When he reached for her chin, she twisted away from him. "I took part of your advice. I didn't mention Uncle Ron to him, but I did tell him that I'd forgiven him for not being there for me all those years."

"How'd he take it?"

"He was fine with it," she said, shaking her head.

"Then it's something I said?" he asked, placing his hand on his chest.

There wasn't a cloud in the sky, but the air seemed to vibrate with coming thunder.

"Rick, it's what you haven't said."

Walking away from him, she knew he would follow by the the suspicious look on his face. Or maybe that was a fearful look. Either way, the morning was about to become a lot more difficult because she refused to push aside the matter with lighthearted bantering, more talk on the fund-raiser, or soul-shattering love-making. Kicking off her sandals, she walked in the ankle-deep aquamarine water lapping gently on the fine sand. Reaching the mangroves, she turned around, bumping into Rick's broad chest. She'd give almost anything to press her face against the comforting mass of warm muscle and steady heartbeat and forget the inevitable for a while longer. But she'd laid her cards on the table with her grandfather, and she was going to do the same with Rick.

"What's this about?" he demanded.

"It's about what Liza and Pappy offered to tell me weeks ago, but I refused to listen to them because I was sure you'd tell me sooner or later. It's about last week when you were in the parking lot at Pappy's. Jiggy let something slip out and everyone there went silent. It's about that beautiful house up there, with no flowers in the planters and no photographs on the walls. It's about you always having an excuse when I mention going out to those little islands out there," she said pointing to the dark green clumps dotting the flat expanse of glimmering aquamarine beyond his front yard. The words rushed out and there was nothing she could do to stop them. Pressing a hand to her chest, she continued. "You told me about Sharon Burke and I understood. Rick, why don't you ever mention your ex-wife to me? What does everyone around here know that I don't?"

"I didn't divorce my wife," he said quietly.

She couldn't have been more shocked if he'd pushed her face first into the shallow water. Staring at him, she waited for the sharp pain in her heart to subside. When she realized it was going to be there for some time to come, she let the next question form on her lips. "You're still married?"

"No."

"But—"

"Bryn, my wife died five years ago. I don't know why I never got around to telling you that," he said as he slipped his sunglasses on. "I guess I've put it all behind me."

No he hadn't. His thin smile and bowed head told her that much and more. With more confusion than she thought she was capable of experiencing, Bryn reached out to take his hand. No matter what unnamed threat his manner presented, Rick Parrish was the man she loved. And right now he needed her understanding. "Lord, Rick, I'm so sorry. I should have just asked it instead of letting my imagination run wild. I had no business blurting this out and jumping all over you about it."

He pulled her close with one arm and walked her back down the beach toward the little dock in front of his house. Reaching for her sandals, he held them against his middle and took a deep breath. He looked as if he were going to say something, but he shook his head instead. "Forget it. It's all in the past."

No it isn't, not for you and me anyway, she wanted to say, but she held her tongue while Rick sat her down on the edge of the dock. Brushing the sand from her feet, he slipped her sandals on while he talked about the obstacle course he and several men were working on for the 10K race. All smiles now, he started describing the planned course in detail. His tone was reminiscent of a moment they'd shared in Key West a few weeks ago. She'd mentioned how little she knew about him and he'd blown off the comment, telling her about a used piano for sale instead.

Neither issue mattered to Bryn. The used piano sat ready and waiting at Pappy's Crab Shack. The obstacle course would be marked in plenty of time for the 10K race next week. The only thing that did matter was the man who still loved Angie.

NINE

As Bryn stapled a spray of metallic stars above the bar at Pappy's, a cheer went up for another finisher in the 10K race in the parking lot below. Feeling anything but cheery, she made a perfunctory stretch to see over the rail. The last thing she wanted was a question about her mood.

"You ought to be down there running in that race, Brynnie," Pappy Madison said as he pushed a section of orange through Miss Scarlett's cage. "I don't need a babysitter."

Bryn looked down from her place on the step-ladder. "I'm not babysitting you. I volunteered along with them to decorate for the ball tonight," she said, waving her staple gun toward the three other people in the bar. "And need I remind you that tonight is also the official reopening of the new and improved Pappy's Crab Shack?"

Turning himself slowly around with the aid of his aluminum walker, he took in every detail of his bar. "Ah, Brynnie," he said in a husky whisper. "You did one hell of a fine job."

Without stopping to think, she said, "I couldn't have done it without Rick's input. He knew what worked and what didn't."

"Where is Rick? I thought I'd see him here this morning."

Keeping his distance from me, she wanted to say, but didn't. Talking about Rick and their relationship was the last thing she wanted now that she knew that Angie Parrish was still a part of Rick's life. Besides, what else could her grandfather tell her? That Rick had loved his wife? She knew that, and she also knew that he *still* loved her.

"Rick's one of the volunteers on the obstacle course over near Johnson's Cove. He's making sure no one drowns in the mud hole." When her grandfather didn't say anything, she checked to see that he was still there. He was. With his face raised in her direction, his thoughtful expression made her suspect he was up to something. "Do you need to see Rick about the Crab Shack? Is everything the way you wanted it?"

Her grandfather's bony shoulders moved in a shrug. "I wouldn't change a thing."

Relieved that he wasn't asking questions about her deteriorating relationship with Rick, she turned back to arrange the clusters of flexible metal stems into sprays of shooting stars. Until a week ago she and Rick had sat out on his deck almost every night, staring at the stars before they went to bed. She would snuggle between his legs, with his arms around her, and they'd take turns with his telescope while he pointed out the constellations. Once she'd asked him what the brightest star was that he'd ever seen.

"You are," he said. "You glow, Miss Madison." Placing a kiss on her cheek, he pointed to a twinkling body high above the darkened horizon. "You light up the night sky like that wishing star."

While she thought about that time, another round of cheering started gathering momentum down in the parking lot. This time she ignored it. Pulling on the shiny metal stems in her hand, she let go, allowing the stars to bounce around in a controlled explosion of reflected light. She'd never look at stars again without listening for the waves lapping against Rick's dock and feeling for Rick's body pressing against her back.

"Brynnie, have you thought any more about my offer?"

Shoving the star-tipped stems against the wooden rack in front of her, she jammed the stapler hard against them. "Please, Grandfather, don't start on that again. You're going to be able to run the Crab Shack without me just fine. Tweed MacNeil promised to tend bar as long as you need him, Susan and Linda are starting back waiting tables tonight, and Rick and Jiggy are here to help you up and down the stairs until you can do it yourself." Raising her hand, she silenced his attempted reply long enough to add, "And you know I already have my own business to run."

"You could live here and run that too," he insisted. "You've been running it from Coconut Key all summer. And I'm an old man. A crippled old man."

When she opened her mouth to speak, he thumped away from her with his walker.

"We'll sit down and talk about it after this fundraiser is over."

Before she could reply, he was halfway across the room to where the mermaid mural was being repainted on the wall opposite the bar.

Calling to him over her shoulder, she said, "You're becoming stubborn in your old age, Grandfather."

"Am not," he said, not bothering to turn around. "Hey, Freddie, I remember my mermaid's, uh, scales being bigger."

"If her 'scales' were any bigger, she'd sink. I think you were in the hospital too long, Pappy," Freddie said.

Everyone in the room hooted with laughter except Bryn. In her case, their beloved Pappy *had* been in the hospital too long. She was beginning to suspect that what was love for her, was simply another affair for Rick. And now that appeared to be winding down.

Already she'd begun to feel him withdrawing from her. Once he'd made a game of sharing long, hot looks with her in a crowded room. Now he looked away the second she tried locking in his gaze. Their easy flow of conversation had dried up to a trickle, leaving her with an anxious feeling that anything she said would sound forced. His work at the marina had suddenly picked up too. At least, that's what he told her when she'd invited him to dinner the night her grandfather came home.

Nothing was the same since she'd asked him about Angie. Nothing except the sex. Through the last week, that hadn't changed, and in fact had somehow increased in intensity. He managed stolen moments with her in out-of-the-way places, with each torrid coupling more passionate than the last. Where or when mattered little to either of them. She went with him without shame, at night in the storeroom below the Crab Shack, during her morning run on the beach at the end of Marina Road, and yesterday, at dawn, inside the cabin of the *Coral Kiss*. She smiled at the last memory; they'd knocked the boxed lunches onto the floor during their lovemaking.

If anything, Rick's physical need for her had deepened to a point where words were unnecessary and only the power of their shared desire mattered. At the end of each encounter he would hold her in a desperate embrace until the outside world called to them.

She tried convincing herself the reason for the change was that their lives had suddenly become hectic with her grandfather's arrival home, activity surrounding the fund-raiser, and Rick's charter business suddenly receiving an onslaught of new clients. Those were all legitimate explanations, but her heart and her head knew there was more to it.

All he'd wanted was his bar back, Rick reminded himself. In the midst of the semiformal ball that signaled the end to the Coconut Key Sports Festival, he unbuttoned the top of his tuxedo shirt and tugged on his bow tie. With the jukebox blasting, Miss Scarlett screeching questionable blessings, and familiar faces milling with new ones, he ought to be the happiest man at Pappy's Crab Shack this evening. Bryn had even had his old chair refinished, and presented it to him in front of Pappy and the fund-raiser committee an hour before the ball began. Easing into the chair, he smoothed his palms along the curved wood while he looked across the room for Bryn. As if his eyes were trained to seek her out, he spotted her immediately, standing by the jukebox admiring someone's blue ribbon. A flood of confused feelings assailed him as he watched her charm the winner of the handicapped division. She hadn't laughed with him like that in days. He could no longer locate the emotional shield he'd always managed to keep over his tender spots in the mix of emotions connected with Bryn. As she moved in and out of the crowd, his insides ached with a strange tension. Bryn wasn't going to be around forever, but, he quickly reminded himself, there was no reason to rush into reviewing his feelings on that subject just yet. Seeing her every day, working with her on the fund-raiser, and making love to her were the only thoughts he allowed into his mind, because he didn't feel right asking for more. Maybe he never would.

Looking at her now, in that incredibly sexy outfit, he felt like whisking her away for a private, blue-ribbon moment of their own. Once he touched her, nothing disturbed their graceful struggle of two becoming one. Nothing. Not even his lingering guilt over Angie's death. Each glorious time he and Bryn came together, his deep feelings of renewal quieted the unfinished feelings surrounding Angie . . . for a while.

But he had to stop lying to himself that all was well with his new lover. He knew Bryn sensed a change, and as a matter of her own survival, she was starting to withdraw from him too. At least that's how he perceived it.

Turning his attention to a basket of hot conch fritters and his beer, he remembered what she had once called him. Coconut Key's local hero. Laughing silently, he bit into a fritter. A coward was more like it. A coward for avoiding her in every way but physically now. Whether or not he could ever figure a way out of the emotional prison he'd placed himself in five years ago, the least he could do was make sure she knew she meant more to him than an object of sexual desire. He ought to be up there on the floor dancing with her. With her warm body pressed against his, and the possibility of making love removed for the next few hours, he knew he could begin to recapture the relaxed mood that used to lead to hours of conversation.

Sliding his beer mug to the center of the table, he started to look for her again. Two executives from the resort on Upper Matecumbe were blocking his view while they admired her cane.

As if she knew he wanted to see her, she moved the two men to one side, giving Rick a clear shot. Bryn used the space to twirl the shiny lacquered walking stick like a baton. Performing a short version of a soft-shoe routine, she ended her dance demonstration by bouncing the cane off the floor and catching it in her opposite hand. While everyone around her applauded, Rick closed his eyes and sent up a thank-you prayer that she'd knotted a long red-starred scarf over the V of her vest.

"Didn't I tell you she was a pistol?"

Rick looked to his right as Pappy Madison, shuffling behind his walker, maneuvered himself into the chair next to his table. "Yes, you did, Pappy," Rick said, reaching for another conch fritter in the red plastic basket near his elbow.

"Loosened up a lot since she arrived. Best thing for her, coming down here to the Keys. The rest of the family's just a bunch of tight-ass grudge-holders."

Despite the din of the blaring jukebox and the mix of happy voices filling the room, Rick was painfully aware of the silence hanging between him and Pappy. Moving forward in his chair, he cleared his throat and reached for his mug of beer. "She pulled all this together pretty damn well," he offered.

Pappy shrugged. "According to Brynnie, she couldn't have done it without you, son."

"I don't know about that."

"Come on, Rick, you've saved the Crab Shack for the second time." He leaned in toward his young friend. "You saved me from drowning in a sea of yellow ruffles, gagging on foreign food, and choking in a necktie every night."

Rick shook his head, refusing to accept the old man's gratitude. Once Pappy got started on Bryn, Rick knew he'd have to think about the last weeks they'd spent together and where they were or weren't going. Glancing over at her again, he realized there was no way he couldn't think about her. Shimmering in her satin costume, she stood out from all the rest of the costumed partygoers. Hell, was that revelation supposed to be a surprise to him? It shouldn't, he thought with immense satisfaction. Buck naked in his bedroom, she shimmered like a vanilla candle at midnight.

"Guess she's been kept pretty busy this summer," Pappy said.

Choosing to ignore his friend's carefully worded implication, Rick leaned back in his chair.

"Yep," Pappy continued, "and on top of this fund-raiser, she tells me she's been running her design business by phone and fax machines. She says it's a lot easier than she thought it would be."

Reaching for another conch fritter, Rick kept his eyes trained straight ahead.

Pappy raised his furry white brows. "Did she tell you I've asked her to stay on and become my partner?"

The conch fritter never made it to his mouth. Staring at the golden fried delicacy as if it were anything but food, he laid it back in the basket. His entire body tensed with possibilities he hadn't allowed himself to think about before this moment. "What did she say?" Keeping his eyes trained toward the salt and pepper shakers, Rick felt Pappy's stare boring into him. "Is she thinking about it?"

"She's thinking about something," Pappy said as he stood up and carefully stepped away from the table.

Pappy's cryptic answer started a cold sweat down Rick's spine. Guilt, hope, and fear churned in his mind as he stared over the railing. Smoke from the barbecue grills wafted through the palms above the rest of the people partying below. Beyond the milling crowd he could see his marina, with all the boats tied up tonight. In the background Miss Scarlett squawked and Martha and the Vandellas sang about nowhere to run. All of these things were familiar, yet tonight they were disjointed bits and pieces from a sensory puzzle that no longer fit together into the picture that was his life. His heart thudded erratically; his brow moistened with perspiration. Nothing felt right. Nothing except his need for Bryn.

Caught in a wave of unnameable emotions, Rick had an overwhelming urge to have her by his side. Slamming his palm on the rail, he cursed under his breath as he pushed up from his chair.

"You'd better not let Miss Scarlett hear you say that, or the whole bar will have to listen to it the rest of the night," Bryn said.

Standing inches from his table, Rick almost bumped into her as he turned around. Her physical presence, coupled with the immediacy of his need to be with her, rendered him momentarily speechless. Instead of trying to locate his voice, he stared at her. Tendrils of golden-red hair had escaped from her top hat and were brushing against her brow and cheeks. A sudden breeze caught them, moving them like a halo of angel's curls around her face.

"Liza wants to see us in the kitchen. She says it's important."

Managing a nod, he followed her through the crowd. As they walked past the hissing fryer filled with conch fritters and through the pantry door, he experienced a jolt of déjà vu. They'd made love in this room. A wild, "anything goes" experience starting with him feeding her lychee nuts from his fingertips and ending with them gasping for air. And for more.

The sight of Liza sitting on a folding chair at a card table in the middle of the pantry, helped him get his mind off the last time he'd been in there. Flipping her steel-colored braids over her shoulders, Liza picked up her calculator and turned it around for them to see.

"I'll give it to you straight. We can't pick up that ambulance until we come up with another six thousand dollars. And we have about forty-eight hours before the price change goes into effect. Then we're looking at five thousand more added to this," she said, tapping the digital display window with her pencil.

"Six thousand dollars," Bryn repeated, removing her hat. "How are we going to come up with six thousand dollars in two days?" Sitting down on an overturned avocado crate, she shook her head, bewildered by the downward turn of events.

"You two will come up with something," Liza said, shoving her paperwork, calculator, and pencil into her bag. "Meanwhile, I'm taking the liberty of scheduling a committee meeting at my house tomorrow at one. You have until then to figure that something out. I'm going out to find the others and tell them to be there."

The solution to the problem came out of nowhere, hitting Rick broadside like an unexpected wave. Momentarily stunned, he let the idea wash through his mind until a smile began forming on his lips. This idea could solve more than the ambulance problem. If the gods were smiling, there was also the chance of a way out of his self-inflicted imprisonment.

"Don't worry, Liza," Rick said moments after she'd left the kitchen. With a burst of energy he turned the card table on its side, collapsed the legs, and stored it behind the door. He quickly folded the chair and slid it next to the table. "Let's dance," he said to Bryn.

Instead of responding to his request, she looked up at him as if he were crazy. "What do you mean, telling her not to worry? How can you be so cavalier about this? We have to come up with six thousand dollars in two days." Pushing off the crate, Bryn turned her back to him and began pacing the narrow room. Rubbing her forehead, she stopped to point at him as he lounged against the doorjamb. "If I didn't know better, I'd think you weren't worried about this money situation in the least."

"If you're certain worrying will help matters, then by all means, go ahead and worry. But right now all I want to do is dance with you to that Smokey Robinson song." He wriggled his fingers at her. "Come on. I haven't held you in hours."

"But Rick," she said, taking his outstretched hand and moving into the comfort of his embrace. "Six thousand dollars? Shouldn't we be talking about how we're going to—"

"Shh." Smiling to himself, he realized the tension inside him had begun disappearing. "By the time we start the committee meeting tomorrow, I'm sure everything will have worked itself out."

"Rick, if you have an idea, I think you ought to tell me, because I don't have one."

Laughing against her curls, he danced her around the pantry. "You have to learn to relax," he said, dipping her dangerously close to the flour can.

"Thanks, Liza, for suggesting we have this meeting at your house. Since the Crab Shack reopened last night, we've lost our meeting site," Bryn said as she settled into a flowery cushion on one of the rattan armchairs.

"I hope you and Rick got to talk about the money problem. Your committee has to deal with this crisis as quickly as possible, Bryn. Once the fun is over, interest tends to quickly lag," Liza said as she passed by Bryn on her way to open the drapes. Brilliant sunshine poured in through the multipaned window facing Liza's front yard and Florida Bay.

Rita covered her eyes and yawned. "Well, sugar, my interest is lagging behind a teeny-weeny headache from that party last night. That was the most fun I've had with my clothes on in years."

"Rita!" Millie whispered, before joining the rest of the group in laughter. "It's true. That semiformal ball idea was unique." Sighing, she looked at Bryn. "I can't imagine what Coconut Key will be like without you."

I can get through this, Bryn told herself, while cold stones dropped one at a time into her stomach. Smiling down at her hands, she took a deep breath. "Maybe we'd better talk about the six thousand dollars needed to purchase the ambulance."

"Shouldn't, ahhh, we wait for Captain Parrish?" Jiggy asked while May Leigh gave him a neck and shoulder massage.

"He said to start without him because he had something he had to do at the bank," Bryn said.

"When, uhhh, did he tell you that?" Jiggy asked as he rummaged through an empty bag of potato chips for a few salty crumbs.

"Earlier," Bryn said, watching a cloud of dust rise from the road outside. *Much, much earlier. He found me in Steadman's All Night Market buying a can of coffee at three o'clock this morning, and took me to Ibis Lane Park, where he made love to me on a picnic table.*

"Then you two did talk? Great, let's hear the idea," Liza said.

Standing up, Bryn had already decided that she wasn't going to mention Rick's peculiar lack of interest in completing the ambulance project. Working with her to find six thousand dollars was the last thing on his mind. In the end it hadn't mattered. She'd taken care of the problem.

Reaching into the deep pockets of her gauzy shirt-waist dress, she felt the rectangle of paper, crisp and big. "I think all of you remember that the second-place finisher in the 10K race was an executive from Conch Castle Resort over on Upper Matecumbe. I spoke to him at the ball last night, and he sounded genuinely interested in our cause. After all, if there's ever a medical emergency over his way, he knows we'll send our ambulance." A murmur of approval floated around her, but was quickly lost within the sound of a car approaching. Glancing over her shoulder, she said, "There's more to tell you, but we might as well wait for Rick."

All eyes were trained on the window behind her, watching a smiling Rick Parrish park his Jeep, vault out of it, and head for the porch. Pushing open the screen door for him, she watched all six feet of his tanned and perfectly toned body heading her way.

"Welcome. You're just in time to hear my announcement."

"Am I?" he asked, wrapping his arm around her shoulders as he walked in and eased the door shut with his foot.

Bryn's heart suddenly lightened at his expression. Compared with his mood lately, his easy attitude was as welcome as a breath of fresh sea air. Even his teasing leer had returned.

"By all means, let's hear your announcement," he said, "because then I have one of my own."

"I had a meeting this morning with the executives from Conch Castle Resort," she said, reaching into the pocket of her dress. Pulling out a piece of paper, she unfolded it, raising it high for everyone to see. "They wrote us a check for six thousand dollars."

A small riot broke out in Liza's living room. While Jiggy danced Liza around the room, Rita attempted twice to high five Millie and May Leigh, then threw up her hands and hugged them both instead.

"Well, Captain, what do you think of Pappy Madison's granddaughter?" Liza asked before bussing Bryn loudly on both cheeks. The two women turned to Rick, while Jiggy continued his dance with the other three.

Shifting his weight to his left foot, Rick leaned away from Bryn and against the door frame. Running his tongue along the edges of his teeth, he appeared to be barely containing his displeasure. "I think she should have checked with me first. The money should come from a source on Coconut Key. You know how these resorts are. Once they get an interest here, they'll—"

"Wait a minute," Bryn demanded, slicing the air with her hand. "The resort is simply helping to pay for the ambulance. Other than community goodwill, the only interest they'll have is if and when they need to request the ambulance for, God forbid, a disaster emergency."

"You should have talked to me before doing this."

"I tried. Remember?" she asked, attempting to regain a light note in her voice. His chin dipped low for an instant as his eyes met with hers. A moment of recognition pulsed through him to her, and that moment of total oneness locked them in a hot look that left her sizzling. A slow smile began stealing across her lips, but when he purposely looked away from her, her cheeks stung with the heat of public embarrassment. Everyone in the room knew, as did most people on Coconut Key, that she and Rick were spending time together on matters other than the fund-raiser.

Taking a calming breath, she tried again. "I understand why you're not enthusiastic about a resort donating the rest of the money, but—"

"Do you?" he said, cutting her off. "We almost lost Coconut Key to that same group."

"You know my grandfather told me. But that was years ago. Can't you give a little on this?"

"Give a little?" he asked, motioning loosely with his hand. "Once people on this key realize where you got the money, they're not going to like the idea. If anyone needs to give here, it's you."

"What are you talking about?"

"I'm talking about you going to Conch Castle and giving them the check back. Bryn, the rest of the money has got to come from here."

"Rick, no one here wants to go through another fund-raiser. And scratching around Coconut Key for donations doesn't make much sense when Conch Castle has already written the check. Besides, we've proven this community cares."

"She's right," Rita said. "This has been fun, but I'm ready to call an end to it. I've got new merchandise in my back room that needed putting out a week ago."

"And I haven't had a scheduled night off in weeks," Jiggy said to May Leigh.

"They don't know me at bingo anymore," Millie said. "Cecilia Barton has taken my seat. I hate when that happens."

As the rest of the group compared stories, Bryn took a step to stand in front of Rick. Shoving a hand to her hip, she spoke with a control that amazed her. "Most of the festival participants were from places other than Coconut Key. And the official sponsors came from as far away as Miami and Key West. You didn't have a complaint about their money. Rick, you've got to back down on this and come to some sort of a compromise here."

"Compromise? These past six weeks have been nothing but compromise."

The hurtful words bit into her, tearing away at that tender center she'd shared with him. She'd been on shaky ground with their relationship for days, and with one quickly delivered retort, he brought her to her knees. Were those deep intimacies they had enjoyed simply hollow pleasures to be put behind them? Was she a fill-in lover until he could find one that was staying around longer? Had Rick pretended to go along with her ideas for the sake of his immediate needs? Damn him. Sex was not all she had to offer.

She'd given him the opportunity to speak about the pain that closed him up in loneliness, but he had declined the offer time and again. Fighting back a quiver of nausea, she tried to hold on to hope. Giving in to hysterical thoughts would be the end of everything. "Rick," she barely managed to whisper, "we are in this together."

"Not for this part. I'm taking care of it, Bryn," he said, pulling a check from his shirt pocket.

"That's your personal check. Why?"

"Just take the other back, Bryn."

There it was. That impatient, demanding tone she hadn't heard in weeks, delivering the order no one would dare challenge. Except her. Her spine straightened as she pushed a shock of loose curls from her forehead. "No, Rick," she said coolly, "I can't do that."

"Yes you can."

She shook her head. "No I can't. I already deposited the Conch Castle check in the ambulance account. This is a cashier's check made out to the ambulance company. I'm leaving in a few minutes to pick it up in Miami."

"Don't do this, Bryn."

Closing her eyes, she continued. "Will you come with me to Miami? Will you finish this with me, Rick?"

She opened her eyes in time to see him fold his check, then shove it in his shirt pocket. Shaking his head, he pushed open the screen door and went out.

The others looked expectantly their way.

"Where's Captain Parrish going?" May Leigh asked, as Bryn caught the screen door before it banged against the door frame. She wouldn't give him the satisfaction of a noisy departure.

"Well, what is happening?" Rita demanded. "What's Captain Parrish so steamed up about?"

"Yes, what have you two decided?" Liza asked.

"I know what I've decided," Bryn said, watching the cloud of dust following him and his Jeep out of the driveway. "Your Captain Parrish can be a very stubborn man."

"Ain't that the truth," Rita said, joining Bryn at the window to watch his speedy departure.

Pulling the last of her pride together, Bryn swallowed back tears. "Well, he can be stubborn until dolphins walk on land, but I made a promise to this community and I intend to keep it." Picking up her purse, she shoved back her hair and forced a shaky smile onto her face. "Anyone want to take the bus up to Miami with me to pick up an ambulance?"

TEN

At eight P.M. Bryn turned on the siren and flashing lights as she drove onto Marina Road and then into Pappy's parking lot. By the time she'd parked the vehicle and turned off the siren, most of the patrons were pouring out of Pappy's stairwell. The swelling crowd and enthusiastic shouts didn't make up for the one missing factor in her moment of triumph. She looked everywhere in the crowd for him and then scanned the faces of those leaning over the upstairs rail. If he was there, he was being careful not to show himself. Soft pain wound around her heart at the thought of him remaining in the shadows.

Liza stepped out of the crowd and lowered her head to the open window of the ambulance. "I know who you're looking for and he's not here, dear," she said, patting Bryn's hand, "but the rest of the com- mittee is."

Bryn wanted to ask why he wasn't there tonight, but she knew the answer. He was staying away from her because of his stubborn need to hold on to the past. She wanted to tell him that the character of Coconut Key was firmly established, and that the donation from Conch Castle Resort couldn't nudge this feisty populace into ever selling out. Rubbing her temples, she tried to bring herself back into the present, yet thoughts of Rick persisted. Being angry with him about his stubbornness would have felt good, but she was already missing him too much for that. Besides, after reassuring him Coconut Key wasn't in danger of changing, the real unresolved issue between them would still be there—his continuing love for Angie.

"You were right going ahead with your plan, dear. You'll see."

See what? What plan? she wanted to ask, but before she could, Liza disappeared back into the crowd. As Bryn strained to find her again, Tweed MacNeil and Jiggy appeared on the brick walkway with Pappy Madison in their arms. May Leigh hurried ahead of them to place his walker securely on the bricks.

"There you go, Pappy," May Leigh said as the old man stood up from the basket of Tweed's and Jiggy's arms.

"Brynnie, it's a beaut," he said, taking small, hard-won steps toward the gleaming new vehicle. "Did Rick let you drive it?" he asked, bracing himself on the walker as he leaned to look in the window of the ambulance. "Where is he? Where's Rick?"

"Grandfather, I drove this all the way from Miami by myself," she said, trying to sound jokingly miffed that he wouldn't have considered that possibility. "I have a proper license."

"What?" her grandfather asked. "Rick didn't go with you? Then where's he been all evening?"

"Rick's at the marina, Pappy," Jiggy said. "He insisted he had to overhaul an engine tonight, but I think he'll take a break to see this. Tweed, why don't you go get him?"

Yes, Bryn thought, *go get him and bring him here so he can make one more cruel remark. Maybe then, when the last shred of hope that we could have worked this out is gone, I can think about what I'm going to do with the rest of my life.*

Stepping from the vehicle, she walked around back to show it off. Opening the doors, she climbed into the interior. "This is your basic ambulance, ladies and gentlemen," she said, pretending to give the sales pitch. Turning back toward the people, she continued pointing out the special features of the model. "We would appreciate it if no one would have a complicated accident until we can afford all the equipment for it."

Rita stuck her head in the back. "You mean all those really fancy-shmancy doodads that we see on that television rescue show?"

"Exactly."

"Hmmm," Liza said, "sounds to me like we should consider having another fund-raiser for those things."

While Rita, May Leigh, and Millie protested, Jiggy took the more dramatic approach. Clutching at his chest, he sank to his knees.

"Somebody, please, get me an ambulance."

The crowd convulsed in laughter as Liza turned toward them, shouting, "Volunteers? Are there any community-minded souls who would like to volunteer for a worthy cause? Ah, Captain Parrish. Perhaps you'd like to volunteer again?"

Bryn's heart skipped a beat when she heard his name. Hope was suddenly surging inside her again, and she didn't care that she was probably certifiably crazy because of it. As optimistic as any child on Christmas morning, she held her breath waiting for his reaction. She knew he wouldn't be interested in participating in another fund-raiser, but once Rick had a good look at the new ambulance, his attitude had to change. No one could remain obstinate in the presence of such an impressive vehicle. So why, she asked herself impatiently, were her hands shaking? The worst was over. Any moment now he would set aside his stubbornness and marvel over the ambulance like everyone else. And if he could do that, anything was possible. Anything. Scooting to the open doors, she looked around for him. Under the flashing light, she met his gaze in an instant that was long enough to send a numbing sensation through her body. She realized suddenly that she wasn't waiting for Rick's reaction to the ambulance. She was waiting for his reaction to seeing her. Within the noisy crowd their stares connected in a vacuum of eery silence.

"Once in a lifetime was enough for me, Liza," he said, looking at Bryn.

Even within the broken light of the ambulance she could see his sober, ungiving expression. Nothing had changed. At the risk of appearing rude, Bryn refrained from pulling the doors closed in his face. Instead, she let his cryptic message sink like acid into her bones. The last of her hope dissolved within her, leaving her with the brutal facts.

He didn't love her.

He would never love her.

He had never loved her.

Once he'd loved Angie, and he was now telling her that one love had been enough for a lifetime. He didn't want to get seriously involved with another woman. Well, she was finally getting the message. They'd had an affair and now it was over. Over. Done with. Behind him. And from this moment on, Rick Parrish was a part of her past too. She'd never bother dragging her pride up to his door again.

"You've been avoiding me all week."

Reaching for her suitcase on the shelf in her closet, Bryn froze. "How did you get in here?"

"Pappy gave me a spare set of his house keys too. What are you doing?"

Jerking the heavy suitcase from the shelf, she let it fall to the floor. "I'm packing my things, Rick. Right after the dedication ceremony I'm leaving." Stepping off the chair, she bent down toward the suitcase, but he kicked it behind him.

"Were you going to leave without seeing me?"

"Of course not," she said, stepping around him and picking up her suitcase. "I would have seen you at the ceremony this afternoon. Unless, of course, you weren't planning to show up for that either."

"Bryn—" he began, but stopped when she pulled away from his outstretched hand.

"To be honest, Rick, I wanted to leave last week after I drove the ambulance down from Miami, but the committee wouldn't hear of it. They insisted I had to be here for the dedication. If you'll excuse me, I have a lot to do before then," she said, flinging the suitcase onto the bed.

He stood by the closet door, watching her unlatch her suitcase. When she refused to acknowledge his presence and started her packing in earnest, he sighed and pinched the bridge of his nose. "Okay, I'll leave you alone now, but be prepared to talk to me this afternoon."

Straightening up, she looked him squarely in the eye. "Is that an order, Captain Parrish?"

"Right now it's a request, but I'll make it an order if you insist," he said without a trace of humor.

When she heard the front door close, tears stung her eyes. Rubbing them away, she turned back toward the bureau. Gathering up her hairbrush and makeup bag, she pitched them into the suitcase, then slammed the lid shut and froze. After a few seconds a strangled sound escaped her throat and she hurried for the door. Grabbing the door frame, she stopped and pressed her forehead against the backs of her hands. "No, you're not going to make a fool of yourself anymore," she told herself. In another few hours this insane need to rush after him would be behind her.

The applause swelled when Bryn walked up the stairs onto the stage behind Liza and the rest of the committee at four o'clock that afternoon. With a shiver of sadness, she realized she was going to miss the group she'd worked with during the summer. For all their wacky traits, they were some of the most decent people she'd ever known. As she began to carefully reminisce, Rita broke into her thoughts with the name of the one person she was trying valiantly not to think about.

"Where's Captain Parrish? He's supposed to be here."

Bryn shrugged, praying wildly that no one would mention his name again.

"Oh, I'm sure Captain Parrish will be along," Liza said, turning from the microphone toward the others. Sliding her reading glasses to the end of her nose, she looked over them at Bryn. "Are you all right, dear?"

All right? Of course she was all right. Hadn't those cucumber slices she'd slapped on her eyelids a few hours ago taken away the puffiness? Had she forgotten how to apply camouflage makeup in only two short months? Was Liza ever going to stop looking at her as if she were a wounded key deer floundering at her door?

Using the last of her shredded patience, Bryn pasted on the perkiest smile she could manage. "I'm fine," she said. Looking to her left and then to her right, she added, "We're all fine, Liza. So let's get on with it."

Settling back against the metal folding chair, Bryn made herself listen to Liza's speech. Several times during the long and often humorous address, Liza slowly scanned the audience.

Fidgeting in her seat, Bryn's mind began wandering again. In a few more minutes this would be over. Before the cake and punch were served, she would be heading for her car. She'd already said her good-byes to her grandfather and the others. And since Rick hadn't bothered showing up, that was one less emotional predicament she had to deal with. At least in front of everyone. What would happen when she was alone in her car was anyone's guess.

"Pssst."

Lost in her thoughts, she barely heard the sound, but there was no way she could miss Rita's nudge to the side of her knee. "What is it?"

"Wake up, sugar. Liza just introduced you."

"What? Why?"

"Damned if I know. Something about your last two months spent in the bosom of this loving community." Standing, Rita joined the rest of the group in a round of applause. "I can't wait to hear what you have to say."

With a sinking feeling in her stomach, Bryn didn't bother hiding her wince. As cochair of the committee she should have known she'd be called on to speak. Unfortunately, she'd allowed her relationship with Rick to overshadow just about everything in her life lately, even her common sense. And now she was going to pay for it.

When the applause died down and Liza had taken her seat, Bryn fiddled with the microphone until she couldn't put off speaking any longer. Looking out over the audience, at her grandfather and then the committee members sitting behind her, she finally spoke. Straight from her heart.

"No one comes away from working on a project like this without learning something new about him or herself."

"I couldn't agree more."

People murmured Rick's name, but the shiver of recognition zipping up her spine would have been enough to confirm his presence if his familiar voice hadn't. From the corner of her eye she could see him several feet to her right, mounting the steps. If he would take a seat behind her, she could get through this.

"So tell us, Bryn, what did you learn about yourself?"

He was publicly challenging her with that teasing intimacy she knew too well. If that weren't confusing enough, he winked at her. Somewhere in this maddening situation, she grasped at her scattering sanity and held on for dear life. Looking out at the audience, she said, "I learned to loosen up."

Stepping halfway behind her, he closed his hands over her shoulders and squeezed them gently. The crowd roared with delight and a few wolf whistles, and he leaned around her to make a disbelieving face and shake his head. Okay, so she was a little tense. What did he expect her to feel like at a time like this? Overcooked pasta?

"Give it back to him, Brynnie!" her grandfather shouted.

The one thing, she quickly decided, that Rick wasn't expecting was a taste of his own medicine. Leaning toward the microphone, she pitched a full bottle at him. "Perhaps you'd like to tell us what you learned, Captain Parrish?" When she started away from the microphone, he held her in front of him.

"Among other things, I learned that backing down occasionally can be a good move."

When she started to step away for the second time, he held her firmly against the front of him. "I also learned that compromise is not a dirty word, except when you make the other person do most of it." Leaning close to her ear, he whispered, "Hold on, this gets better." Straightening, he maneuvered her to one side and spoke into the microphone.

"I have to apologize to Bryn for giving her such a hard time. I put off starting this project, dragged my feet through most of it, and then I couldn't seem to let go of it. I hope she forgives me." Pausing for a perfectly timed punch line, he smiled and said, "Because I'd hate to be on Pappy's bad side now that the Crab Shack's reopened."

When the laughter died down, Rick continued. "I'd also like to let Liza know that she can take a break from committee organizing, at least where ambulance equipment is concerned. I'm donating the necessary funds to pay for the equipment."

Thunderous applause drowned out Bryn's response, but he didn't mind. She could tell him later. When they were alone and he had told her everything else. Raising his hand for silence, he asked, "Did I see a key lime pie with my name on it around here somewhere?"

Liza stepped up to the microphone. "You did, Captain. Let's all adjourn to the Crab Shack."

After a half dozen thank-yous, Liza and the rest of the committee streamed off the platform, leaving Rick and Bryn alone. He watched her strain for something to say, wishing she wasn't still so uncomfortable with him. After a few seconds she tucked a lock of hair behind her ear and looked up at him.

"That was very kind of you to donate your money for the equipment. I'm sure people here are extremely grateful for your generosity. I really need to get going. Good-bye, Rick."

"Hold on, there," he said, pulling her back from the steps. "Since I'm in such a kind and generous mood, I have something for you too."

"What?" she asked, studying him with suspicion.

"A boat ride on the *Coral Kiss.*"

He saw her eyes light with surprise, then dim with doubt.

"You told me you never use that boat for—well, that you only use it for business."

"I've changed my mind."

She gave him an indecisive look, then shook her head. "I'd better not. I have a long drive ahead of me."

His arm shot out, blocking her way down the steps. "Uh-uh."

"What are you doing?" she asked incredulously.

Cocking his chin, he ran his tongue over the edges of his teeth. "Sorry, but I'm pulling rank on you. You have a boat to catch."

"Rick, no. If I go with you, we'll—"

"What will we do?" he asked, his heart hammering against his rib cage. Moving toward her, he cupped her face in both hands. "Make love? Say it, Bryn."

"No," she said, avoiding his smile as she attempted to push him out of the way. "I'd rather be forced to watch the weather channel with my eyes glued open."

"Once we're back, you can do what you want," he said, taking her hands and holding them against his chest. "Right now we have a few more things to talk about."

"You cannot make me get on that boat if I don't want to."

"Of course I can," he said, leading her down the stairs and into the palm grove. "Captain's orders."

She stopped struggling when she spotted Liza and Pappy leaning over the upstairs rail, waving at them. "I'm only going with you because I don't want to make a scene in front of these people. I don't think this is funny. You ought to be ashamed of yourself—"

"I am," he said pleasantly. "Very ashamed. I thought I'd developed sufficient charm to get you on the boat with a simple request, but I was wrong. I've had to order you on."

She didn't say another word until they were out of the marina and nearing what had to be Alligator Reef.

"Where are you taking me?" she demanded, her arms crossed tightly against her chest. Her rigid posture had her swaying unsteadily with the boat's movement.

"Right here."

Bryn stared across the blue-green water to where it lapped in lacy wavelets against a short stretch of sandy beach. Her arms dropped open at the sight. All summer long she'd looked out from Pappy's at the dozen or so small islands, wondering what they were like up close. Now she knew, and the beauty of the place ate at her insides. Was that August Moon Key? Was that perfect piece of paradise where he used to bring Angie? "What's it called?"

"It doesn't have a name," he said, lowering the anchor.

"There are still unnamed places left on this planet?" she asked, while breathing a secret sigh of relief that it wasn't August Moon Key.

Before she knew how it happened, he had pulled her into his arms and was kissing her in an all-out attempt at seduction. And he was doing one heck of a job. "I missed you," he murmured, pressing his hands against the small of her back. With the warmth of his breath on her cheek and his scent mixing with the essence of the sea breezes, she almost forgot that her problem couldn't be wiped away with his touch.

"No, I can't do this," she said, pushing away from him. "Stay right there. I don't want you to kiss me."

"Liar."

"Okay, so maybe I do, but I'm not going to let you make love to me."

"We'll see about that."

"Would you stop being so cocky about this sexual chemistry between us," she said, punching the bulkhead with her fist. "You always have to have things your way in the end, don't you? Well, this time you're not going to get what you want."

"What's that?"

"Me," she said, stabbing at her breastbone with her finger. Narrowing her eyes at his smile, she continued. "There's supposed to be more to a relationship than multiple orgasms."

"Go on," he said, urging her with a dip of his chin.

"There's supposed to be honesty. Openness. Trust."

"I agree."

"Well, why haven't you been honest and open with me? Why haven't you trusted me to handle the truth?"

"About what?"

"About your wife." She didn't know what to expect, but it wasn't the warm and understanding smile he gave her.

"Because I'm a jerk."

"That may be true, but it doesn't explain why you never told me about her. Or why you got so upset when I refused your money for the ambulance. The two are connected, aren't they?"

He nodded. "Oh, yes. They're connected." Slipping his corded sunglasses from around his neck, he placed them on the shelf next to the wheel. "Bryn, my wife was pregnant when she died. The doctors had told her she needed to be in a hospital for the last few months. She loved our life on Coconut Key and put off leaving until the last possible day the doctors would allow. Even then she wanted to prolong it. She asked me to take her out on this boat one more time. I didn't have to take her, but everything seemed so right that day." Shrugging, he shoved his fingers through his sun-streaked hair. "There wasn't a cloud in the sky that morning. She said she felt fine. We planned to drive up to Miami later." He paused to look out a few hundred yards across the water. Lifting his chin, he said, "We had a picnic over there on August Moon Key . . . and then around two o'clock all hell broke loose. Everything that could go wrong, went wrong. She started bleeding. The radio wouldn't work. And the nastiest storm blew up here from Cuba. When I finally got her to the marina, I couldn't get the ambulance to come for her because it was being used to tend to the victims of a six-car pile-up on one of the bridges, along with all the other ambulances in the area." He raised his hands, then wrapped his arms around his waist as he shifted his weight against the bulkhead. Staring out at August Moon Key, he said, "She and the baby died. It was a little boy. I held him."

"Oh, Rick," she said, holding her hands to her mouth. His silent stare told her he wasn't finished, and that she must let him before she could reach out to him. "I'm so sorry," she managed to whisper.

Running his hand along the smooth white fiber-glass, he paused for a long while before looking at her again. "After the hurricane the next year, I used Angie's life insurance to help Pappy and the others fix up the mess. What was left sat in the bank until last week, when Liza told us we needed more money for the ambulance. I got it in my head that using Angie's insurance money to pay for the ambulance was the only chance I was ever going to have to rid myself of this guilt. But you beat me to it with that check from Conch Castle."

She'd never imagined torment such as his, and that she had added to it in even a small way pained her. What hot tears weren't choking Bryn, slipped down her cheeks in blessed relief. "If only you would have talked to me."

"My mind was jumbled with guilt over Angie and the baby, my responsibility to the committee, and every emotion imaginable where you're concerned. Rather than allow myself to accept that something wonderful was happening between us, I kept telling myself all we had was great sex. I knew you'd even-tually leave, and I stupidly thought I could weather that transition and then go on with my life." He shook his head, laughing silently. "Boy, did I have that all wrong."

"You did?"

"Yes. When it finally sunk in that you were leaving, I did some hard soul-searching and realized I'd already started putting the agony and guilt behind me."

"When did you start?"

"When you came to me and said you were making a big mistake redoing Pappy's. I knew how much those renovations meant to you, and yet you knew when to give up and admit you were wrong. I don't think I've ever admired anyone as much as I did you at that moment." Taking her in his arms, he kissed her softly on her lips. "You lit up the sky that night. It took me until this week to realize that you gave me back my future too. Bryn, I want you to stay and share it with me."

Pressing her fingers against his chest, she licked a tear from her lips. "Sounds like you're not going to back down on this order, Captain Parrish."

"Order? Hell no," he said as he stroked her tears away with his thumbs. Framing her face in his hands, he kissed her again with a profound gentleness that made her breathless. "This isn't an order. It's a humble request from the man who loves you. Please, promise me—"

"I'm not leaving you. And I'm not leaving Coconut Key," she said, shaking her head emphatically. "I love you."

"Wait, I'm not finished."

"You're not? But I—"

"Hell no. I'm just getting started," he said as he sat her down and pressed her back along the padded bench.

Much later, while they watched the sunset, she sat with her back against his chest as he nibbled on her shoulder. "I'm going to hold you to your promise that you'll marry me, but are you sure you're up to the rest of the list?"

Rubbing her cheek against his arm, she laughed softly. "Every one, Captain Parrish, and some we haven't thought of yet."

THE EDITOR'S
CORNER

Since the inception of LOVESWEPT in 1983, we've been known as the most innovative publisher of category romance. We were the first to publish authors under their real names and show their photographs in the books. We originated interconnected "series" books and established theme months. And now, after publishing over 700 books, we are once again changing the face of category romance.

Starting next month, we are introducing a brand-new LOVESWEPT look. We're sure you'll agree with us that it's distinctive and outstanding—nothing less than the perfect showcase for your favorite authors and the wonderful stories they write.

A second change is that we are now publishing four LOVESWEPTs a month instead of six. With so many romances on the market today, we want to provide you with only the very best in romantic fiction. We know that you want quality, not quantity, and we are as committed as ever to giving you love stories you'll never forget, by authors you'll always remember. We are especially proud to debut our new look with four sizzling romances from four of our most talented authors.

Starting off our new look is Mary Kay McComas with **WAIT FOR ME**, LOVESWEPT #702. Oliver Carey saves Holly Loftin's life during an earthquake with a split-second tackle, but only when their eyes meet does he feel the earth tremble and her compassionate soul reach out to his. He is intrigued by her need to help others, enchanted by her appetite for simple pleasures, but now he has to show her that their differences can be their strengths and that, more than anything, they belong together. Mary Kay will have you laughing and crying with this touching romance.

The ever-popular Kay Hooper is back with her unique blend of romantic mystery and spicy wit in **THE HAUNTING OF JOSIE**, LOVESWEPT #703. Josie Douglas decides that Marc Westbrook, her gorgeous landlord, would have made a good warlock, with his raven-dark hair, silver eyes, and even a black cat in his arms! She chose the isolated house as a refuge, a place to put the past to rest, but now Marc insists on fighting her demons . . . and why does he so resemble the ghostly figure who beckons to her from the head of the stairs? Kay once more demonstrates her talent for seduction and suspense in this wonderful romance.

Theresa Gladden proves that opposites attract in **PERFECT TIMING**, LOVESWEPT #704. Jenny Johnson isn't looking for a new husband, no matter how many hunks her sister sends her way, but Carter Dalton's cobalt-blue eyes mesmerize her into letting his daughter join her girls' club—and inviting him to dinner! The free-spirited rebel is all wrong for him: messy house, too many pets, wildly disorganized—but he can't resist a woman who promises to fill the empty spaces he didn't know he had. Theresa's spectacular romance will leave you breathless.

Last but certainly not least is **TAMING THE PIRATE**, LOVESWEPT #705, from the supertalented Ruth Owen. When investigator Gabe Ramirez sees Laurie Palmer, she stirs to life the appetites of his buccaneer ancestors and makes him long for the golden lure of her smile. She longs to trade her secrets for one kiss from his brigand's lips, but once he knows why she is on the run, will he betray the woman he's vowed will never escape his arms? You won't forget this wonderful story from Ruth.

Happy reading,

With warmest wishes,

Nita Taublib

Nita Taublib

Deputy Publisher

P.S. Don't miss the exciting women's novels from Bantam that are coming your way in August—**MIDNIGHT WARRIOR**, by *New York Times* bestselling author Iris Johansen, is a spellbinding tale of pursuit, possession, and passion that extends from the wilds of Normandy to untamed medieval England; **BLUE MOON** is a powerful and romantic novel of love and families by the exceptionally talented Luanne Rice. *The New York Times Book Review* calls it "a rare combination of realism and romance"; **VELVET**, by Jane Feather, is a spectacular novel of danger and deception in which a beautiful woman risks all for revenge and love; **THE WITCH DANCE**, by Peggy Webb, is a poignant story of two lovers whose passion breaks every rule. We'll be giving you a sneak peek at these terrific books in next month's LOVESWEPTs. And immediately following this page, look for a preview of the exciting romances from Bantam that are *available now!*

Don't miss these extraordinary books by
your favorite Bantam authors

On sale in June:

MISTRESS
by Amanda Quick

WILDEST DREAMS
by Rosanne Bittner

DANGEROUS TO LOVE
by Elizabeth Thornton

AMAZON LILY
by Theresa Weir

"Power, passion, tragedy, and triumph are Rosanne Bittner's hallmarks. Again and again, she brings readers to tears."
—*Romantic Times*

WILDEST DREAMS
by

ROSANNE BITTNER

Against the glorious panorama of big sky country, award-winning Rosanne Bittner creates a sweeping saga of passion, excitement, and danger . . . as a beautiful young woman and a rugged ex-soldier struggle against all odds to carve out an empire—and to forge a magnificent love.

Here is a look at this powerful novel . . .

Lettie walked ahead of him into the shack, swallowing back an urge to retch. She gazed around the cabin, noticed a few cracks between the boards that were sure to let in cold drafts in the winter. A rat scurried across the floor, and she stepped back. The room was very small, perhaps fifteen feet square, with a potbellied stove in one corner, a few shelves built against one wall, and a crudely built table in the middle of the room, with two crates to serve as chairs. The bed was made from pine, with ropes for springs and no mattress on top. She was glad her mother had given her two feather mattresses before they parted. Never had she longed more fervently to be with her family back at the spacious home they had left behind in St.

Joseph, where people lived in reasonable numbers, and anything they needed was close at hand.

Silently, she untied and removed the wool hat she'd been wearing. She was shaken by her sense of doubt, not only over her choice to come to this lonely, desolate place, but also over her decision to marry. She loved Luke, and he had been attentive and caring and protective throughout their dangerous, trying journey to get here; but being his wife meant fulfilling other needs he had not yet demanded of her. This was the very first time they had been truly alone since marrying at Fort Laramie. When Luke had slept in the wagon with her, he had only held her. Was he waiting for her to make the first move; or had he patiently been waiting for this moment, when he had her alone? Between the realization that he would surely expect to consummate their marriage now, and the knowledge that she would spend the rest of the winter holed up in this tiny cabin, with rats running over her feet, she felt panic building.

"Lettie?"

She was startled by the touch of Luke's hand on her shoulder. She gasped and turned to look up at him, her eyes wide with fear and apprehension. "I . . . I don't know if I can stay here, Luke." Oh, why had she said that? She could see the hurt in his eyes. He should be angry. Maybe he would throw her down and have his way with her now, order her to submit to her husband, yell at her for being weak and selfish, tell her she would stay here whether she liked it or not.

He turned, looked around the tiny room, looked back at her with a smile of resignation on his face. "I can't blame you there. I don't know why I even considered this. I guess in all my excitement . . ." He sighed deeply. "I'll take you back to Billings in the morning. It's not much of a town, but maybe I can find a safe place for you and Nathan to stay while I make things more livable around here."

"But . . . you'd be out here all alone."

He shrugged, walking over to the stove and opening the door. "I knew before I ever came here there would be a lot of lonely living I'd have to put up with." He picked up some kindling from a small pile that lay near the stove and stacked it inside. "When you have a dream, you simply do what you have to do to realize it." He turned to face her. "I told you it won't be like this forever, Lettie, and it won't."

His eyes moved over her, and she knew what he wanted. He simply loved and respected her too much to ask for it. A wave of guilt rushed through her, and she felt like crying. "I'm sorry, Luke. I've disappointed you in so many ways already."

He frowned, coming closer. "I never said that. I don't blame you for not wanting to stay here. I'll take you back to town and you can come back here in the spring." He placed his hands on her shoulders. "I love you, Lettie. I never want you to be unhappy or wish you had never married me. I made you some promises, and I intend to keep them."

A lump seemed to rise in her throat. "You'd really take me to Billings? You wouldn't be angry about it?"

Luke studied her face. He wanted her so, but was not sure how to approach the situation because of what she had been through. He knew there was a part of her that wanted him that way, but he had not seen it in her eyes since leaving Fort Laramie. He had only seen doubt and fear. "I told you I'd take you. I wouldn't be angry."

She suddenly smiled, although there were tears in her eyes. "That's all I need to know. I . . . I thought you took it for granted, just because I was your wife . . . that you'd demand . . ."

She threw her arms around him, resting her face against his thick fur jacket. "Oh, Luke, forgive me. You don't have to take me back. As long as I know I *can* go back, that's all I need to know. Does that make any sense?"

He grinned. "I think so."

Somewhere in the distance they heard the cry of a bobcat. Combined with the groaning mountain wind, the sounds only accentuated how alone they really were, a good five miles from the only town, and no sign of civilization for hundreds of miles beyond that. "I can't let you stay out here alone. You're my husband. I belong here with you," Lettie said, still clinging to him.

Luke kissed her hair, her cheek. She found herself turning to meet his lips, and he explored her mouth savagely then. She felt lost in his powerful hold, buried in the fur jacket, suddenly weak. How well he fit this land, so tall and strong and rugged and determined. She loved him all the more for it.

He left her mouth, kissed her neck. "I'd better get a fire going, bring in—"

"Luke." She felt her heart racing as all her fears began to melt away. She didn't know how to tell him, what to do. She could only look into those handsome blue eyes and say his name. She met his lips again, astonished at the sudden hunger in her soul. How could she have considered letting this poor man stay out here alone, when he had a wife and child who could help him, love him? And how could she keep denying him the one thing he had every right to take for himself? Most of all, how could she deny her own sudden desires, this surprising awakening of woman that ached to be set free?

"Luke," she whispered. "I want to be your wife, Luke, in every way. I want to be one with you and know that it's all right. I don't want to be afraid any more."

DANGEROUS TO LOVE
by Elizabeth Thornton

"A major, major talent . . . a genre superstar."
—*Rave Reviews*

Dangerous. Wild. Reckless. Those were the words that passed through Serena Ward's mind the moment Julian Raynor entered the gaming hall. If anyone could penetrate Serena's disguise—and jeopardize the political fugitives she was delivering to freedom—surely it would be London's most notorious gamester. Yet when the militia storms the establishment in search of traitors, Raynor provides just the pretext Serena needs to escape. But Serena is playing with fire . . . and before the night is through she will find herself surrendering to the heat of unsuspected desires.

The following is a sneak preview of what transpires that evening in a private room above the gaming hall. . .

"Let's start over, shall we?" said Julian. He returned to the chair he had vacated. "And this time, I shall try to keep myself well in check. No, don't move. I rather like you kneeling at my feet in an attitude of submission."

He raised his wine glass and imbibed slowly. "Now you," he said. When she made to take it from him, he shook his head. "No, I shall hold it. Come closer."

Once again she found herself between his thighs. She didn't know what to do with her hands, but he knew.

"Place them on my thighs," he said, and Serena obeyed. Beneath her fingers, she could feel the hard masculine muscles bunch and strain. She was also acutely aware of the movements of the militia as they combed the building for Jacobites.

"Drink," he said, holding the rim of the glass to her lips, tipping it slightly.

Wine flooded her mouth and spilled over. Choking, she swallowed it.

"Allow me," he murmured. As one hand cupped her neck, his head descended and his tongue plunged into her mouth.

Shock held her rigid as his tongue thrust, and thrust again, circling, licking at the dregs of wine in her mouth, lapping it up with avid enjoyment. When she began to struggle, his powerful thighs tightened against her, holding her effortlessly. Her hands went to his chest to push him away, and slipped between the parted edges of his shirt. Warm masculine flesh quivered beneath the pads of her fingertips. Splaying her hands wide, with every ounce of strength, she shoved at him, trying to free herself.

He released her so abruptly that she tumbled to the floor. Scrambling away from him, she came up on her knees. They were both breathing heavily.

Frowning, he rose to his feet and came to tower over her. "What game are you playing now?"

"No game," she quickly got out. "You are going too fast for me." She carefully rose to her feet and began to inch away from him. "We have yet to settle on my . . . my remuneration."

"Remuneration?" He laughed softly. "Sweetheart, I have already made up my mind that for a woman of your unquestionable talents, no price is too high."

These were not the words that Serena wanted to hear, nor did she believe him. Men did not like greedy women. Although she wasn't supposed to know it, long before his marriage, her brother, Jeremy, had given his mistress her *congé* because the girl was too demanding. What was it the girl had wanted?

Her back came up against the door to the bedchamber. One hand curved around the door-knob in a reflexive movement, the other clutched the door-jamb for support.

Licking her lips, she said, "I . . . I shall want my own house."

He cocked his head to one side. As though musing to himself, he said, "I've never had a woman in my keeping. Do you know, for the first time, I can see the merit in it? Fine, you shall have your house."

He took a step closer, and she flattened herself against the door. "And . . . and my own carriage?" She could hardly breathe with him standing so close to her.

"Done." His eyes were glittering.

When he lunged for her, she cried out and flung herself into the bed-chamber, slamming the door quickly, bracing her shoulder against it as her fingers fumbled for the key.

One kick sent both door and Serena hurtling back. He stood framed in the doorway, the light behind him, and every sensible thought went out of her head. Dangerous. Reckless. Wild. This was all a game to him!

He feinted to the left, and she made a dash for the door, twisting away as his hands reached for her. His fingers caught on the back of her gown, ripping it to the waist. One hand curved around her arm, sending her sprawling against the bed.

There was no candle in the bed-chamber, but the lights from the tavern's courtyard filtered through the window casting a luminous glow. He was shedding the last of his clothes. Although everything in her revolted against it, she knew that the time had come to reveal her name.

Summoning the remnants of her dignity, she said, "You should know that I am no common doxy. I am a high-born lady."

He laughed in that way of his that she was coming to thoroughly detest. "I know," he said, "and I am to play the conqueror. Sweetheart, those games are all very well in their place. But the time for games is over. I want a real woman in my arms tonight, a willing one and not some character from a fantasy."

She turned his words over in her mind and

could make no sense of them. Seriously doubting the man's sanity, she cried out, "Touch me and you will regret it to your dying day. Don't you understand anything? I am a lady. I . . ."

He fell on her and rolled with her on the bed. Subduing her easily with the press of his body, he rose above her. "Have done with your games. I am Julian. You are Victoria. I am your protector. You are my mistress. Yield to me, sweeting."

Bought and paid for—that was what was in his mind. She was aware of something else. He didn't want to hurt or humiliate her. He wanted to have his way with her. He thought he had that right.

He wasn't moving, or forcing his caresses on her. He was simply holding her, watching her with an unfathomable expression. "Julian," she whispered, giving him his name in an attempt to soften him. "Victoria Noble is not my real name."

"I didn't think it was," he said, and kissed her.

His mouth was gentle; his tongue caressing, slipping between her teeth, not deeply, not threateningly, but inviting her to participate in the kiss. For a moment, curiosity held her spellbound. She had never been kissed like this before. It was like sinking into a bath of spiced wine. It was sweet and intoxicating, just like the taste of him.

Shivering, she pulled out of the embrace and stared up at him. His brows were raised, questioning her. All she need do was tell him her name and he would let her go.

Suddenly it was the last thing she wanted to do.

AMAZON LILY

by the spectacular

Theresa Weir

"You must be the Lily-Libber who's going to San Reys."

The deep voice that came slicing through Corey's sleep-fogged brain was gravelly and rough-edged.

She dragged open heavy-lidded eyes to find herself contemplating a ragged pair of grubby blue tennis shoes. She allowed her gaze to pan slowly northward, leaving freeze-framed images etched in her mind's eye: long jeans faded to almost white except along the stitching; a copper waistband button with moldy lettering; a large expanse of chest-filled, sweat-soaked T-shirt; a stubbly field of several days growth of whiskers; dark aviator sunglasses that met the dusty, sweaty brim of a New York Yankees baseball cap.

Corey's head was bent back at an uncomfortable angle. Of course, Santarém, Brazil, wasn't Illinois, and this person certainly wasn't like any case she'd ever handled in her job as a social worker.

The squalid air-taxi building was really little more than a shed, and it had been crowded before, with just Corey and the files. But now, with this man in front of her giving off his angry aura . . . She couldn't see his eyes, but she could read enough of his expression to know that she was being regarded as a lower form of life or something he might have scraped off the bottom off his shoe.

She knew she wasn't an American beauty. Her skin was too pale, her brown eyes too large for her small face, giving her a fragile, old-world appearance that was a burden in these modern times. People had a tendency to either overlook her completely or coddle her. But his reaction was something totally new.

The man's attention shifted from her to the smashed red packet in his hand. He pulled out a flattened nonfilter cigarette, smoothed it until it was somewhat round, then stuck it in the corner of his mouth. One hand moved across the front of the faded green T-shirt that clung damply to his corded muscles. He slapped at the breast pocket. Not finding what he was searching for, both of his hands moved to the front pockets of the ancient jeans that covered those long, athletic legs. There was a frayed white horizontal rip across his right knee, tan skin and sun-bleached hair showing through. Change jingled as he rummaged around to finally pull out a damp, wadded-up book of matches.

"Damn," he muttered after the third match failed to light. "Gotta quit sweating so much." He tossed the bedraggled matchbook to the floor. Cigarette still in his mouth, his hands began a repeat search of his pockets.

Corey reached over to where her twill shoulder bag was lying on a stack of tattered *Mad* magazines. She unzipped a side pocket and pulled out the glossy black and gold matches she'd been saving to add to her matchbook collection.

He grabbed them without so much as a thank-you. "That's right—" he said, striking a match, "you girl scouts are always prepared." He shook out the match and tossed it to the floor.

"Are you Mike Jones?" She hoped to God he wasn't the pilot she was waiting for.

"No." He inhaled deeply, then exhaled, blowing a thick cloud of smoke her direction.

"Do you know when Mr. Jones will be here?" she asked, willing her eyes not to bat against the smoke.

"*Mister* Jones had a slight setback. He was unconscious last time I saw him." The man read the ornate advertisement for the Black Tie restaurant on the match cover, then tucked the matches into the breast pocket of his T-shirt. The knuckles of his hand were red and swollen, one finger joint cracked and covered with dried blood.

"I found Jones in a local cantina, drunk out of his mind and just itching to fly. Had a little trouble convincing him it would be in his best interest if he stayed on the ground. My name's Ash—Asher Adams, and it looks like I'll be flying you to the reserve. If you still want to go."

Corey pushed her earlier thoughts to the back of her mind. "Of course I still want to go." She hadn't come this far to back out now.

"You want my advice?" He pulled off the navy-blue cap and swiped at his sweating forehead before slapping the cap back over shaggy brown hair. "Go back home. Get married. Have babies. Why is it you women have to prove you're men? You come here thrill-seeking so you can go home and be some kind of small-town hero. So your whole puny story can be printed up in a little four-page county paper and you can travel around to all the local clubs and organizations with your slide presentation, and all your friends can ooh and aah over you."

Corey felt heated anger flushing her face. She pressed her lips together in a firm, stubborn line.

What an obnoxious boor! In her years as a social worker, she'd never, *never* come across anyone like him. And thank God for that, she fumed.

Asher Adams took another drag off his cigarette, then flopped down in the chair across from her, legs sticking out in front of him, crossed at the ankles. "Go back home," he said in a weary voice. "This is real. It isn't some Humphrey Bogart movie. This isn't Sleepyville, Iowa, or wherever the hell you're from—"

"Pleasant Grove, Illinois," she flatly informed him. "And I don't need your advice. I don't want it." Who did this overbearing man think he was? She hadn't taken vacation time to come here and be insulted by an ill-tempered woman-hater. And he talked as if she planned to settle in the jungles of Brazil. There was nothing further from her mind.

She zipped her bag and grabbed up her cream-colored wool jacket. "I'd like to leave now."

And don't miss these fabulous romances
from Bantam Books, on sale in July:

MIDNIGHT WARRIOR
by the *New York Times* bestselling author
Iris Johansen
"Iris Johansen is a master among
master stoytellers."
—*Affaire de Coeur*

BLUE MOON
by the nationally bestselling author
Luanne Rice
"Luanne Rice proves herself a
nimble virtuoso."
—*The Washington Post Book World*

VELVET
by the highly acclaimed
Jane Feather
"An author to treasure."
—*Romantic Times*

THE WITCH DANCE
by the incomparable
Peggy Webb
"Ms. Webb has an inventive mind
brimming with originality that makes
all of her books special reading."
—*Romantic Times*

OFFICIAL RULES

To enter the sweepstakes below carefully follow all instructions found elsewhere in this offer.

The **Winners Classic** will award prizes with the following approximate maximum values: 1 Grand Prize: $26,500 (or $25,000 cash alternate); 1 First Prize: $3,000; 5 Second Prizes: $400 each; 35 Third Prizes: $100 each; 1,000 Fourth Prizes: $7.50 each. Total maximum retail value of Winners Classic Sweepstakes is $42,500. Some presentations of this sweepstakes may contain individual entry numbers corresponding to one or more of the aforementioned prize levels. To determine the Winners, individual entry numbers will first be compared with the winning numbers preselected by computer. For winning numbers not returned, prizes will be awarded in random drawings from among all eligible entries received. Prize choices may be offered at various levels. If a winner chooses an automobile prize, all license and registration fees, taxes, destination charges, and other expenses not offered herein are the responsibility of the winner. If a winner chooses a trip, travel must be complete within one year from the time the prize is awarded. Minors must be accompanied by an adult. Travel companion(s) must also sign release of liability. Trips are subject to space and departure availability. Certain black-out dates may apply.

The following applies to the sweepstakes named above:

No purchase necessary. You can also enter the sweepstakes by sending your name and address to: P.O. Box 508, Gibbstown, N.J. 08027. Mail each entry separately. Sweepstakes begins 6/1/93. Entries must be received by 12/30/94. Not responsible for lost, late, damaged, misdirected, illegible or postage due mail. Mechanically reproduced entries are not eligible. All entries become property of the sponsor and will not be returned.

Prize Selection/Validations: Selection of winners will be conducted no later than 5:00 PM on January 28, 1995, by an independent judging organization whose decisions are final. Random drawings will be held at 1211 Avenue of the Americas, New York, N.Y. 10036. Entrants need not be present to win. Odds of winning are determined by total number of entries received. Circulation of this sweepstakes is estimated not to exceed 200 million. All prizes are guaranteed to be awarded and delivered to winners. Winners will be notified by mail and may be required to complete an affidavit of eligibility and release of liability which must be returned within 14 days of date on notification or alternate winners will be selected in a random drawing. Any prize notification letter or any prize returned to a participating sponsor, Bantam Doubleday Dell Publishing Group, Inc., its participating divisions or subsidiaries, or the independent judging organization as undeliverable will be awarded to an alternate winner. Prizes are not transferable. No substitution for prizes except as offered or as may be necessary due to unavailability, in which case a prize of equal or greater value will be awarded. Prizes will be awarded approximately 90 days after the drawing. All taxes are the sole responsibility of the winners. Entry constitutes permission (except where prohibited by law) to use winners' names, hometowns, and likenesses for publicity purposes without further or other compensation. Prizes won by minors will be awarded in the name of parent or legal guardian.

Participation: Sweepstakes open to residents of the United States and Canada, except for the province of Quebec. Sweepstakes sponsored by Bantam Doubleday Dell Publishing Group, Inc., (BDD), 1540 Broadway, New York, NY 10036. Versions of this sweepstakes with different graphics and prize choices will be offered in conjunction with various solicitations or promotions by different subsidiaries and divisions of BDD. Where applicable, winners will have their choice of any prize offered at level won. Employees of BDD, its divisions, subsidiaries, advertising agencies, independent judging organization, and their immediate family members are not eligible.

Canadian residents, in order to win, must first correctly answer a time limited arithmetical skill testing question. Void in Puerto Rico, Quebec and wherever prohibited or restricted by law. Subject to all federal, state, local and provincial laws and regulations. For a list of major prize winners (available after 1/29/95): send a self-addressed, stamped envelope entirely separate from your entry to: Sweepstakes Winners, P.O. Box 517, Gibbstown, NJ 08027. Requests must be received by 12/30/94. DO NOT SEND ANY OTHER CORRESPONDENCE TO THIS P.O. BOX.